Chronicle of the Lake

by

Roderick Saxey

Written about 1972
Copyright 2023 by Roderick Saxey
Selah, WA
ISBN 978-0997018110
Library of Congress Control Number: 2023909033

For all who love mountains and valleys,
forests and flowers,
rivers and lakes,
and chess.

Contents

Chronicle of the Lake takes place in a fantasy world. Any resemblance between the people and places in this story and those in the real world is purely coincidental and highly gratifying.

Prologue

Dr. Miller was waiting in the shade of the maple tree when Chris Lowie hopped from his truck in front of the research station.

"You're late," said the older man. He pointed to the other folding chair. "Sit down. Black or white?"

Chris sat. "Sorry, Joe, I got carried away with my work. Black." They began to set up the chessmen on the card table between them. "We began a new level today."

"Hmm. Anything interesting?"

"I'll say. Some of the finest obsidian points I've seen."

Dr. Miller muttered, "You archaeologists. You always talk in superlatives."

"Here, look at this and tell me it isn't beautiful." Chris pulled from his pocket a long piece of stone with a sharpened double edge and fluting down the middle.

"I'll admit it's nice." The biologist rubbed his finger. "Still sharp, too. How old is it?"

"It's from a period just before the Tarmian Empire—about 3,000 years ago.

"A long time ago."

"Yes." Chris ran his hand through his wavy blonde hair. "Things have changed a lot since then."

Dr. Miller handed back the stone and moved his knight.

"Aha," said the archaeologist, "a Reti opening. Trying some razzle-dazzle today."

Miller frowned. "We'll see."

The plastic armies progressed around the chessboard. After a while the old biologist took a stained pipe from his breast pocket and filled it with tobacco. Waiting for Chris's move, he sat wreathed in smoke, staring out at the placid lake in the hollow between the mountains. Forests stretched away from it in all directions. The distant gleam of a city could be seen in the clear air, with smaller towns and villages scattered along the shore. A large, rocky island jutted out of the middle of the lake. It looked like a misplaced temple. Nearer at hand was the swamp that surrounded the research station's landing.

Dr. Miller wrinkled his brown forehead and drew on his pipe,

"No, I don't think that's quite right, Chris."

"What do you mean 'not right'? Of course, it's right. You made the same move yourself just a minute ago."

"Not your move. What you said."

"What did I say?"

"That things have changed a lot since prehistoric times. I'm not sure I believe that."

Chris leaned back in his chair. "How can you say that? From stone knives to factories? Everything has changed tremendously."

"Oh, sure, we've come a long way technologically. But there is a lot more to the universe than technology."

"True enough," said Chris, looking again at the stone knife. "But they had a very different way of life from ours too, different beliefs, different worries, different everything. Just suppose you and I had lived then, at the beginning of civilization, Man was just beginning to find himself."

"Yes, and probably he was a little surprised at the kind of creature he was. Man was reaching out," said the biologist, "trying to find his place in the universe. I wonder if he has succeeded?"

"We certainly seem to have found a place."

"True, but is it the place we belong in, or have we fooled ourselves somehow?"

Chris frowned. "That is philosophical—different department. We can never really know the answer to that." His frown turned to a smile, "but we can imagine."

"I'm not sure my imagination is that good."

"You underestimate yourself, Doctor. You are a biologist, a scientist; I am an archaeologist, an historian. All that training must be good for something. Let's imagine what we would have been doing 3,000 years ago. What would have been our place in the universe then?"

They both leaned back in their chairs. "Very well," said Dr. Miller. "Let's imagine."

CHAPTER 1

Lake People

The grey boar turned and saw young Ratu. It charged, yellow tusks glistening with spittle, a dull red gleam in its eyes. Ratu held his spear ready near his right temple, his thick black hair whipping in the wind. His legs trembled as he watched. He felt he had become a sapling on the shore and was about to be blown to slivers by a storm from the lake. The boar was not twenty feet from him—he had to do something!

Suddenly a lean figure sprang from the bush beside him and thrust a spear deep into the creature's breast. The beast charged at its assailant, throwing him over its back and into the soft grass. But it was too late. The boar heaved a great sigh and collapsed into the dust.

Ratu ran to the side of his rescuer, who had already risen and was brushing himself off, "Lorim, are you hurt?"

"No. No fat pig can hurt a tough old man like me," he said, running his fingers through his grey beard and straightening his green tunic. "That was yours, though. Why didn't you kill it?"

Ratu looked down. "I do not know. I couldn't move. I . . ." He broke off.

The young man looked at his mentor and saw the familiar look of disappointment on his face. They had been together nearly a year, living in a hut set a little apart from the rest of the village. Ratu was receiving special instruction prior to the great succession at which he would become Ratu-tani, the chief priest.

Lorim, eldest of the Oak set of Eel clan, was his instructor in lore and ritual, including the killing of the sacred boar. Lorim's eyes were like watery pools that twinkled with knowledge. But they did not twinkle now. They reflected disbelief and despair for Ratu and his people.

"Surely tomorrow will be better," ventured the young man.

"I hope it is so. You know the law. Tonight, we ask the chief priest to offer sacrifice for you." He thought for a moment and added, "And where prayer does not succeed, perhaps magic will."

Lorim quickly tied the boar's legs to his spear and lifted it up onto Ratu's shoulder. Ratu could feel the animal's warmth lingering beneath its fur. They turned and vanished into the forest, leaving no trace but some torn leaves and a spot of red where the great beast had died.

The village hummed with activity as the two returned. The workday was drawing to a close, and any projects to be completed must be done quickly so that the evening meal could be finished before dark and the coming of the night spirits. A dozen fishing canoes moved gently with the current in the middle of the broad lake.

Beyond them loomed Tani, the island, the earth's navel. It stood like a sentinel, observing the villagers' every act, giving its approval or disapproval as necessary through its prophet-priests, watching carefully that the incessant struggle between light and dark not be won, lest nature's harmony be disrupted. Ratu looked, gave the sign; and walked on.

A group of children playing at the shore saw their approach and ran to them. Each wore a breechcloth. They smiled mischievously in greeting. Their mothers sat nearby, weaving baskets of various shapes and sizes from the reeds that grew thick in the fen where the dwellings were built. Juveniles Ratu's age stood knee-deep in the water, pulling at plants or hunting frogs and other small animals to eat. A band of women came with berries and fungus from the forest to the northwest. They sang as they arrived at the shore, deposited the treasures in canoes, and paddled out to their homes, built on log pilings a few yards into the swamp.

Ratu and Lorim put their prize into a round bark made of reed and driftwood. The old man grunted. "First we go to Kanu-tani." He shot a glance at Ratu.

They paddled among the houses, moving toward the center where the chief priest's house stood, larger than the rest and decorated with bones of various animals and enemies. Had it been late winter, when the lake was low, they might have gone straight to the building; summer brought the lake close to the floors, so they had to maneuver carefully to keep from jostling against the supports.

They tied their little boat to a post by the main entrance. A woman reached down and helped them onto the landing. "Welcome, Lorim," she said pleasantly. "It is many days since last you came to us." She did not greet the younger man.

"Indeed, it is. I have been in the forest, teaching the future one."

"So," she said, folding her arms gracefully. "Kanu-tani is in the inner room. Ngana-han is with him."

"It is well," the old man replied.

The house was dark. It had one small window, high in the south wall, and the door in the east wall. They picked their way past piles of furs and tools toward the curtain that divided the main room from the tani's living quarters. In the corner could be seen heaps of wicker baskets and small wooden boxes from which strange smells arose.

The woman parted the curtain and two men stood to greet the visitors. The tani and the han were men in their prime, strong and handsome, yet lines of care showed on their faces. They had held their offices nearly ten years, and they were glad they would soon be succeeded by their younger relatives. They would then move on to the first council of elders.

Kanu-tani threw back the boar-skin cloak that hung from his shoulders. He shook Lorim's hand and kissed his brow. A blue stone bounced with other ornaments on a string around his neck. "Lorim, welcome. How goes the training of my sister's son?"

Lorim paused before answering. "Tani, I have come to speak to you about this. But first, Ngana-han, long though it is since the tani and I have rested beneath the same roof, longer still it is since you and I have passed a pleasant evening together."

The han smiled. "True, Wise One. Your duties have taken you from us, as is the will of the gods."

Everyone ignored Ratu. He seated himself in a corner behind Lorim and averted his eyes from the two warriors. It was improper for an adolescent to gaze on such men. Instead, he stroked the soft beaver on which he sat and counted the repairs that had been made in the woven reed walls.

After some idle chatter, Lorim got to the reason for his visit. "Kanu-tani, in the training of your sister's son I have found him very receptive to herbal lore, also the sacred knowledge of the beginnings, and to the lesser rites. Yet in other things I have found him to have weakness." He paused again.

"Today we hunted the boar. The young one had seen it thrice before, yet as the pig charged, he found himself unable to move. He would have been torn to pieces had I not come to his aid. Never have I seen such a thing—to be so afraid. A little fear is normal, but this!" Lorim held up his hands in exasperation.

The tani and the han exchanged looks. Lorim continued, "The spirits are at work; only they have such power. I have brought the pig. Take it tonight to the sacred island and offer it to the god. The succession must continue. If not, it will pass out of your family to a different lineage. And who knows but that one day, if Ratu's sister should have a son, he would claim the priesthood. Then there would be a division in the tribe, and strife over who should lead in the holy order."

The tani paused before answering. He closed his eyes as if in deep thought, then said, "It is well you have told me of this, Lorim. I will go to the island tonight and seek the gods' help. I shall ask the lake as well, for she has limitless powers."

The men talked a little longer, about relatives and friends and the more humorous events of the day. When they rose to leave, Kanu-tani withdrew a nasturtium leaf from a small leather bag that hung round his waist. He rubbed it on the hands of his two adult guests and murmured a spell, while Ratu silently moved into the other room where the woman sat cracking nuts. The others followed shortly.

After the dead boar had been transferred to the tani's boat, Ratu and Lorim climbed into their own and began the homeward journey. They hurried, for dusk had come while they were inside. The shadows of the houses and the trees on shore lay black about them. Away to the east the mountain tops shone bright in the last sunlight. In the west a long bright slash of evening color cut across the darkening sky.

Lorim's house stood beyond the edge of the village, not far from shore. On the landing they found a basket of hot bread and fish and a smaller one of fresh berries, left there by Ratu's sister. Lorim's wife had died of an illness some years before, so usually his mother's brother's daughter provided food for him, but as the new tani's teacher he shared the food given Ratu by his mother's people.

After their meal Lorim built a small fire on the box of sand in the middle of the house. Then once again he told the story of creation to his young pupil. He had barely begun when Ratu interrupted him. "Lorim, thank you for what you did."

"Asking the tani for help? Anyone can do that for anything."

"No, I mean for not telling him about the other times. You know." He looked away, embarrassed.

"Yes, I know. You are special, Ratu, and will be a great tani one day. The spirits desire to destroy you. Why that is so I do not know, but they have great power. Only greater power can defeat them. Kanu-tani will summon that power. Then you will see the evil spirits flee and your own self-will return." He paused. "But all this will not teach you what you must know."

He continued his story. "After the creators had borne earth they nourished her for many years with the light of stars through a great tube. This tube joined earth at the place called Tani. When earth was old enough the tube was removed and a great stone placed over the spot where it had been, and a spirit put in the stone to guard it. But the stone was not tight, and so earth's blood seeped out all around, making the great lake. When the creators saw this they sent other spirits into the lake to stop the leak and seal the hole forever.

"Things were well with the universe for a long time. Earth gave birth to forest and to many spirits, good and bad. And then the bad spirits banded together to attack Tani and dislodge the stone. They thought earth would die and they would have power over all the other spirits. It was a terrible struggle. There were lights in the sky and thunder, and the rocks cracked and broke under the strain. So great were the powers that were unleashed that earth groaned and flexed, and so were created the mountains that surround the valley.

"But when the creators saw all this pain, they were sad. They saw too that Tani and the good spirits became weaker with every day that passed, while the evil spirits grew stronger. They said, 'The only merciful thing to do is kill earth, and all spirits and rocks and trees and living things. Such misery and suffering cannot be endured.'

"It was then that they heard a voice. A very small voice it was, and at first, they were not sure where it came from. But they looked down at the lake, and there by the shore stood Han.

"Han called to the creators and begged them not to destroy the earth and all things. But they said they must, for the forces of good were growing weak, and evil strong, and if the good were subdued even the creators would be in danger. Then they asked what manner of creature Han was, for they did not recognize him. He replied, 'I am a son of earth. There are many of us in the forest, hiding from the terrible fight. If you will spare earth and all things from destruction, some of us will come live on the lake. We will feed the good spirits and serve them, that they will have strength to continue the struggle against evil.'

"The creators considered this suggestion and decided to give Han a chance. So it happened that Han and his brother, their families and friends moved onto the lake. They went to Tani too, where a huge blue stone had been placed as a token of the agreement. It is there that sacrifices of fruit and fish and sacred boar are made each midwinter's day. This is how good is nourished. You are a descendant of the wife of the brother of Han, Ratu. It is to you that the responsibility for maintaining the covenant and all the important facts of lore and ritual will fall. Be happy in your duty, for it is through us that the universe is preserved, and harmony maintained."

Lorim leaned back against the wall. Ratu yawned and looked out the little window that opened toward the east. Lights burned on the island, and the blackness of the lake surrounded it. The sight reminded Ratu of the special sacrifice being made on his behalf. He thought of Han, the courageous.

The two said good night, and the young man crawled onto his pallet by the east wall as Lorim heaped ashes on the fire to preserve the coals until morning. Ratu pulled his furs up about his shoulders and he closed his eyes, but he did not sleep. His mind was wide-awake.

Everything had been easier before. He had known for a long time that spirits longed to seize and destroy, or at least dishonor him, but his position as future tani kept the other children from thinking too badly of him, and the tani protected him. When they swam out into the lake, he always stayed closer to shore, near the fen. He was a good shot with the spear and sling and had a reputation among the boys as a hunter, but when confronted with a large or dangerous animal in the woods, his courage fled.

And he had a mortal fear of being captured by the forest people. When the rest of the village was busy trading on the rare days they appeared, Ratu slinked behind the houses, out of sight. He did not know why such fears troubled him. They never mattered much until now. Now he must prove himself. He must be the heir of the brother of Han.

CHAPTER 2

Forest People

There was one thing the others feared that he did not, however. Ratu smiled as he thought about It. Even the tani, who had power over darkness and was known to travel at night to the island, would stay tonight after the sacrifice, huddling with his assistants near the campfire, reciting ancient songs to fortify their courage.

But Ratu had no fear of darkness. His parents had once taken him with them into the forest to gather apples from a grove some distance from the village. The forest people were hostile at the time—there is never more than an uneasy peace between the two groups—and his father should not have gone without warriors to guard them. They were attacked on the road home. Somehow Ratu escaped and hid himself in the brush by the path. He was thoroughly lost.

Night found him in the same spot. At first, he was terrified by the darkness but as the evening wore on, he discovered that there was nothing to fear. He began to wander about, feeling like a spirit gliding between the trees, creeping from beneath bushes, a breath among living things. He watched the stars and drew strength from them, listened to the hum and beat of creation, began to *know* the universe. The souls of all creatures were laid bare to his gaze in the faint moonlight, and he thought himself like the gods.

The people were amazed to see him step from the woods early the next morning. That he had survived the night as well as the forest people's attack was a miracle beyond hope, evidence of the protection which the gods had given the heir of Han's brother. They pummeled him with questions, but he did not tell of his new-found power.

Many times since, Ratu had stealthily left the village to wander the hillsides and meadows, watching the stars and moon and feeling the powers of earth. The tiny window showed only one of the myriad stars of the universe. It shone in on the tired young man in Lorim's house as he drifted off to sleep.

Dew covered the oak, maple, and fir trees as they wove their way through the forest in the gray morning light, past hill and rock, bush and stream. Lorim led, Ratu following wearily. The pupil did not see the point of starting so early, when sleep still clouds the eyes and muscles do not cooperate. Lorim would say nothing of their destination or of their secret purpose; only that they must journey far into the forest people's land and would not return until the following day or so.

Gradually the way led upward, toward the mountains looming in the west. Dampness filled the air, along with the scents of rotting needles and leaves and tiny summer flowers beside the path. The sun rose, and with it a thick mist in all parts of the valley. At last, they halted under a large old oak, a patriarch of the forest. There they rested. Lorim took from his waist pouch a slice of dried apple and gave it to Ratu, who accepted it gratefully.

"We have come far and fast, Lorim, and are deep in the wood. Can you not tell me where it is we are going?" asked Ratu.

"It is good for you to learn patience. Yesterday I said we would use prayer and magic to help you conquer the spirits that give you fear. Prayer was made last night. Now is the time for magic. We journey to Dorag, the sorcerer, who lives at the foot of the western mountains. It is not far, now. Do you fear this?"

"No. I wonder, though. Can a sorcerer of the forest people have greater power than the tani?"

The teacher glanced warningly at his companion. "Know this secret! There are many forces in the world, both for good and evil. Even before Han, they existed, some before earth herself, even before her spirit stirred. Many are fading now, but not all are forgotten. Dorag dwells in the forest, true, but he is not of its people. He is the child of no man and serves no master but the gods who rule us all."

Lorim looked cautiously around at the trees and shrubs. A wren sat perched on a currant bush a few yards away. The travelers made the sign, for they had heard many tales of evil lurking in the dark wood. They passed into the shadows of the rising sun, more silent than the south wind that brushed the treetops.

They arrived at the home of Dorag shortly before noon. He dwelt in a cave deep in a high cliff face, the first upthrust of the western mountains. Though the cliff rose some seventy feet above the valley floor and the cave entrance was dark and large, Dorag had cleverly arranged rock and bush in the entrance to create the illusion that the cave had no depth. Ratu thought Lorim was most certainly mistaken when he announced they had arrived and pointed to the cliff face before them. But Lorim walked to a large stone by the entrance and rapped three times with his staff.

A short old man appeared as suddenly as if dropped from the sky. His small black eyes peered from beneath bushy brows at the visitors. Shaking his beard, he said, "What do you want, disturbing a poor man's peace so?"

"Forgive us, Dorag. It is on a matter of great urgency that I come. Do you not recognize me?" asked Lorim.

"Of course, Lorim the Wise is not forgotten. But I have problems of my own. Why should I listen to yours? And why do you bring a stranger to my home?" He pointed a crooked finger at Ratu.

"This is Ratu, soon to be the new tani. He should know you and you him."

"So. And you want me to help him somehow, I assume." The sorcerer looked at the young man with narrowed eyes, then turned to Lorim. "How much?"

"Two fish per week for a year. Prime catch and large. Here is one as token of my word." He undid a small pack he had slung about his shoulder and held up a good catfish.

The sorcerer's eyes glittered. "Three and it's a deal."

"Two and three, alternate weeks."

"Done!"

The travelers followed their host past the rock and bushes and found themselves in a large cavern, The ceiling of the cave was high above them, beyond the flickering light of the torch fastened into the wall on their left. In the middle of the room was a dark pool, fed by unseen streams bubbling up from the earth's center. Ratu drew in his breath; he had never seen such a place before. Dorag led them past the pool, down rough-hewn steps, and into a side corridor which led to a smaller room in the doorway of which was hung a worn and faded bearskin.

On one side of this room stood a long table covered with neat stacks and piles of herbs and berries and roots—and other things the origin of which Ratu could not guess. On the other side stood a bench heaped with furs and pillows. Their host bade them sit, then brought seedcakes, goat's milk, and dried fruit. When they had eaten, they discussed the problem to be solved.

Ratu forgot many of the details of that afternoon and night. He slept a little while Dorag mixed tiny plants and dark earth in the pot that hung over the great fire he built near the entrance. Then the tired young man had to sit up straight while the sorcerer rubbed ointments on his limbs, drained blood from his arm, and recited ancient chants and formulas. Though he tried to take mental note of all that was done, Ratu often found himself simply staring into the flickering light and the cloud of smoke that gathered on the ceiling of the cave. Finally, Dorag sat back on his leather stool and heaved a great sigh. Was he finished?

He shook his head. "I cannot continue."

Lorim sprang up. "Why? What is the matter?" he asked.

"I need fresh porcupine quills to make divine signs on the boy's back to protect him from future attacks by the spirits. But the sun is long asleep, and I am too weary to hunt in the evil darkness. We must wait."

"Is there no other way? The succession is not far off, and there is still much to be learned."

Dorag thought a while. "Well, perhaps." He peered at Lorim's side. "A friend's knife, if specially prepared, might be used."

Lorim took his fine obsidian blade with the narrow flutings over which many spells had been said and handed it the old man. This was great magic indeed, for knives are powerful and sacred things. Dorag rubbed leaves on it, singing softly about Han's brother, then looked around him and went into the large cavern. Ratu looked apprehensively at his teacher.

"Do not fear. He is a master," Lorim said.

Dorag returned after a few moments with the knife in his right hand. A dark liquid dripped from it. In his left hand was a grey, stringy substance.

"Cobwebs. To stop the bleeding," Lorim explained.

Then came the agony. Seven cuts on the right, seven on the left, an arch overall, and a triangle in the middle to represent Tani. Ratu's back flamed. He tried to think of swimming in the cool lake water, but always the thought of burning sand intruded. He bit his lip.

"Lie down, now. It is finished, but for one detail we can complete before you leave. Rest now."

Ratu lay among the furs on the bench but could not rest. His whole body burned with fire like the sun that cannot be quenched, his tongue swelled, and pain filled his mind, chasing out other thoughts. Dimly he heard the other two talking, but he knew only his own body.

It seemed like days later when the sorcerer's withered old hand touched his shoulder and he said, "Come. It is time you eat."

Their fare was the same as before, with the addition of a pale wine that soothed Ratu's throat. When they were filled, Dorag stood. "I have done what you wanted. You must leave now. The second day is nearly half spent, and I'll not have you lagging until it is too late. You can still reach the lake by nightfall."

He led them through the curtain and the cavern to the cave entrance where they had first seen him the day before. The sun was high in the southern sky. The world was so bright that they squinted in the brilliance. There was a narrow meadow at the cave entrance. The forest began a few yards beyond, and far past the forest, twinkling like an eye of the earth, stretched the lake, dark, cool, and deep. In its center was the island.

"Young man, your protection is not complete," said the old sorcerer. "It will never be complete. Of all powers in the universe, one of the greatest was given to man at his birth by earth. It slumbers in most, though perhaps not so soundly in you as in others. Draw on it for your strength and you will succeed in your tasks.

"One thing more," he added, holding up a small white crystal suspended on a leather thong. "This is from earth's heart. Wear it always and it will give you courage."

He hung the crystal around the young man's neck and Ratu felt warmth where the stone touched his chest. At that moment, far below them in the depths of the forest, they heard a dull boom. It was like the beat of a drum or the voices of the gods when they shake the ground.

Dorag gazed toward the lake as if in a trance, then started. "You must make haste. The spirits of evil work mischief among the forest people. Even now they have set upon your village at the time of the great exchange, with no respect for the ancient tradition of peace in trade. Hurry!"

The old man turned and vanished into the face of the mountain. His guests opened their mouths as if to say thanks, but he was gone. Lorim whispered, "Come," and they hurried off into the forest. Even as they did so they saw a plume of white smoke rise from where their village lay.

Kalad sat with Josse, his teacher, on a rock near the shore of the lake, listening to Josse recite the history of his people from the first han to the present. Soon would be the great succession and he would be the han, and would lead his people in peace and war, together with the tani. It will be good working with Ratu, he thought, letting his mind wander. They were old friends, though of different clans. Ratu had been perhaps a little aloof from the other boys, but Kalad had been able to reach him, and they had shared many of their thoughts and feelings.

The young man nodded his head, causing his long black hair to fall into his face. "Kalad," said his teacher, "pay attention. You will have to know all this for the succession."

The future han knew of Ratu's lack of fear of the evil of night, so it did not worry him that no one had seen Ratu and Lorim return from the forest yesterday. It was their secret. A remarkable thing, he thought, that boy who never showed any great strength in swimming or great power with animals should possess power over darkness, even more than Kanu-tani.

Above Kalad a flock of gulls flew out toward the island, the sky behind them a clear blue, with only a few billowy clouds. A breeze made ripples in the lake water. The villagers went about their normal routines, except that the men were gathering extra fish, baskets, and other handicraft at the edge of the wood to trade with the forest people who were expected soon.

They arrived at noon. The two peoples were distant kin and resembled each other closely; all had dark skin, dark hair, and broad foreheads. They were scantily dressed, rarely more than a loincloth and a tunic, except in winter when other skins were worn. Each carried a great spear, and most had a knife. They looked at the trade pieces carefully. The bargaining began. But something was peculiar about the exchange today. It was as if some half-expected and ominous possibility hung over the event.

Kalad watched from his place at Josse's side. At last, the visitors stood up. From somewhere a great drum sounded one low note, and from the woods behind them sprang forty or fifty more forest men, shouts on their lips, spears in their hands. A cloud passed in front of the sun and a chill filled every heart as the warriors swept down upon them. The women clutched their children to their breasts and ran for the boats to make for open water. The men reached for their own weapons to make a stand. But it was no use. Before they could begin to fight several had been killed. The rest could do nothing but surrender. Only a few boatloads escaped.

Kalad, too, was captured. Josse was not so fortunate. He ran, only to have a spear pierce his back, The han was also dead, as well as his personal guard. The enemy took faggots from the cooking fires on the shore and threw them on the grass roofs of the nearby houses; they flamed like dry tinder. Far away, on the island, Kanu-tani saw the smoke rise. He dropped the knife he held over the fish of sacrifice. Doom had come.

A rough hand snatched at young Kalad, pushing him along with the other captives. Made to carry the plunder so recently their own property, they were herded off into the forest toward a distant village. Kalad could only think, muttering to himself, "So the power is gone, and this is why Ratu and Lorim did not return at sunset."

CHAPTER 3

Mystics

The great blue stone towered twice the height of a man, its white patches and black and purple veins speckled with yellow. It glistened in the firelight. Ratu had seen it twice before—at the ceremony ten years ago when his age set was initiated and last summer when he and Kalad were set apart to become tani and han. It all seemed eons ago to Ratu. His back stung and his legs ached from running.

When they had arrived at the village shortly before dusk, all but three of the houses were burnt to the ground and a half dozen bodies were strewn on the ground. Kanu-tani, his assistants, and some women, children, and old men who had escaped the attack in boats were there, searching among the wreckage for anything they could salvage; all were wailing at the terrible destruction.

Now Ratu lay stretched on the sand, looking up at the great stone, wondering what was to become of his people. At the foot of the stone was a rough-hewn altar, stained with the blood of many sacrifices, worn with much use. Huts stood against the rock sides of the island on the north, south and east; the west was open to permit a view of the far end of the lake where dwelt the people of Han. Han! Kalad was to become the next han.

Ratu looked up at the new moon, struggling against the starlight around it. When it was full the ceremony was to be performed. He, tani, Kalad, han, leaders of their people. But what people? Disaster had struck. Their homes were destroyed, their ways shattered. What hope was there of surviving to see things set right?

There was one chance, thought Ratu. He looked at the others. Most had gone to bed and mercifully found relief in sleep. Lorim nodded drowsily, Kanu-tani soon did the same. No one saw the silent shape move stealthily to the boats on the beach an hour later. This shadow pushed a small, round vessel out into the lake and began paddling quietly toward the west. As he did so the wind sighed and the ripples on the surface spread away to where the forest touched them in the distance. The island waited as if expecting change.

When Ratu reached the trees he stopped and turned to look back at the lake. He shook his head in disgust. This is no good, he thought, I don't even know where I'm going. All I know is that they live somewhere in there. And what will I do if I find them? Fight without even a spear of my own? He hung his head and started to paddle back.

Then far above him in the sky a star fell across his path, showering sparks and lighting the valley. Upon his breast the crystal seemed to jump and grow warm. It was the work of the gods. He turned back toward the forest. He did not know what was in store for him, but he hurried on his way. The gods wished him to continue.

As he ran through the forest Ratu felt the darkness wrap itself around him, became aware of presences he never noticed in daylight. The beasts cowered when they felt his spirit pass but did not see his body nor the faint moonlight shining in the hair which streamed out behind him. He was like the wind in the meadows. The gods led him.

Even with this speed it was dawn before he reached the village of the forest people, deep in the wood, shaded by great, dark firs that grew there. He hid beneath a bush where he could watch and wait.

It was a nice place, thought Kalad, if only we could be at peace and be friends. The houses were built soundly of wood and grass, with mud to fill in the spaces and keep out the draft. And the people seemed well fed. It seemed strange not to see water lapping at the footings, though, or to be able to see Tani in the distance.

The forest people did not keep their prisoners tied, for they knew no one would escape from here, certainly not at night. On the morning of the second day the chief assigned them to different families to help with village chores.

"We once were brothers," said the old man gruffly. "Your leaders were wrong to take you away from the deep wood and the ancient gods. But you will learn to work in the fields and to gather on the hillsides as we do, as your ancestors did. We will be one people again."

Kalad's mind wandered as the chief spoke. He just said the same things over again anyway; it was the same speech he gave when they first arrived. What difference did it make? With no one to serve the island and the lake, evil would prevail, men would be forgotten once more, and the universe would be destroyed; the ancient lore said so.

The prisoners weeded all that day in fields of yams, grain, beans, and other plants they weren't familiar with, then were fed and put into a hastily erected lean-to for the night. Most slept after a few moments, but Kalad remained awake, listening to the night noises.

He suddenly realized the noises had changed; last night there had been many crickets just outside their hut, but tonight only those in the distance could be heard. He looked cautiously out the small door cut into the side of the house and saw squatting there a familiar figure, though somehow different and larger.

"Ratu, it is good to see you! I thought you dead!" he whispered.

"I feared the same for you, my friend." They clasped arms and Kalad crawled out into the dark so as not to awaken the sleepers.

They exchanged stories, then Kalad whispered, "What of the future, Ratu? Is there a chance?"

"A chance, yes, though small. There are not enough of us to fight the forest people, but I have an idea. I need your help." The conspirators crept away.

Toran, chief of the forest people, was very weary when he went to bed. "If only they knew what burdens rest upon the shoulders of their leader," he grumbled to his wife, "they would not complain so much.

It was a grave decision to attack the lake people during trading; had it been left to me we would still be at peace. But young Roagan and Haran and the others, those fiery young men, troublemakers with silly notions about changing traditions and restoring more ancient ways, they were the ones who forced me to agree in the conference house. Too bad they are elders now."

Toran had been chief long enough to know to bend with the wind when necessary, to yield when the will of the people demanded it. So now they could expand the village a little. But who would they trade with for fish and other things from the lake? Should they move the village to the shore or make expeditions there for supplies? And if they did something like that, who conquered whom? Are the lake people now forest people, or the forest people becoming lake people? Just try to tell Roagan that, though. Ah, the ignorance and short-sightedness of youth!

Finished with his reflections, the chief was sleeping soundly when a commotion outside awakened him. Voices and shouts and alarms in the middle of the night were unusual and strange, for only spirits were abroad in the darkness. He picked up the great staff of office that rested by his bed and rushed into the open space between the huts. All the men and even many of the women were there in the dim light of the evening watchfire, now burned low in the middle of the square. Some had their spears at the ready. Others were still too bleary-eyed to know what to do or what was happening.

All stared at the creature that stood at the edge of the wood, more illuminated by the stars than by the fire. Its long dark hair hung in strings upon its neck; its countenance was pale. A ghost it was, clad only in loincloth and thin green tunic covered in grass and leaves. There was a faint gleam in its eyes and an aura of darkness about its person. Upon its breast hung a white stone that glittered in the starlight and flickered when its wearer spoke.

"Listen," cried the creature in the voice of a young man. "The people of the forest have angered the gods by violating their oaths of friendship with the lake people. I am a spirit of the lake and have come with a message for you."

Toran stepped in front of his people. His legs quivered beneath him, but he spoke bravely. "I am Toran, Chief. Why have you come, and what is your message?"

"I warn you of your doom."

A deep voice called out of the crowd, "And why should we heed a liar of the night? What but an evil spirit is abroad at this hour?" It was Roagan, brash as ever.

Before the chief could speak the spirit raised the thick staff it carried and pointed it at Roagan. "Beware!" it roared. The spirit stamped the staff on the ground, shaking the leaves that still clung to it.

"You must return the lake people to their land tomorrow, help them rebuild their homes, and swear eternal peace with them. So have the gods decreed!" As he spoke the remaining night noises completely died away and only his voice could be heard, rushing like rainwater.

Toran licked his lips and looked at the ground. "And if we do not as you demand?"

"You will be destroyed!"

The chief thought a moment. How could this be anything but what it seemed? What could a poor chief of men do against a messenger of the gods? Then Roagan jumped in front of the chief, anxious and angry, hunger in his eyes.

"Surely you do not believe this imposter!" he cried. "It is a trick of the lakers. Even in defeat they try deceit and lies and seek the help of evil spirits and ghosts."

The spirit cut off the next sentence. "Silence! I speak the words of the gods. If you do not believe me, let this be a sign. Look!" He pointed his staff toward the other end of the village.

There stood the council house, where the business of the people was discussed by the elders, decisions were made, and the law decreed. As they watched, smoke billowed from it and flame leapt into the sky.

For a moment it seemed the afternoon sun had come too soon. The dry old building snapped and cracked, its destruction sure.

Some of the forest people threw themselves on the ground and wailed, others were dumbfounded and stood with their mouths drooping. A few had the presence of mind to run to the nearby pool to fetch water to douse the flame. Toran stood rooted to the spot. Was there any choice in what he must do? Surely even Roagan wouldn't object now. He also had seen the power of the gods who alone command the sun. He turned to address the spirit, but it had vanished into the night, leaving only confusion and indecision behind.

It had taken much washing in the stream to remove all the white clay and leaves from Ratu's face, neck, hands, and arms. Now he hid among the ferns and azaleas at the edge of the forest near the lake and surveyed the scene.

The forest people were most apologetic and worked hard to rebuild the lake people's village. They left after the third day, swearing their oaths to the elders and the tani—there would be no han until the end of the month. When they were gone, Ratu came from his concealment, feeling quite self-conscious about the stares and exclamations that greeted him.

Lorim looked at the thin young man and tears came to his eyes. "Ratu!" he cried, throwing his arm around his pupil. The people gathered around them, and a murmur went up as they praised the lake and Tani for preserving the heir of the priest.

"Didn't Kalad tell you?" asked Ratu.

"Tell me what?"

Kalad had rejoined his people two days earlier and now stood nearby, a grin splitting his face, "Perhaps later. There will be much time for stories."

They prepared a feast to celebrate their salvation. As they ate, Kalad and Ratu looked at the island on the lake and thought of the coming succession, when all the age-sets advanced to match their years and they would receive their offices.

"We will lead our people well," said Kalad.

"Tani through us and we will prosper," replied Ratu.

They stood awhile in reverent silence. Above them fluffy white clouds bloomed and collided and swept away to the north. The forest whispered, the water danced, nature was at ease. Ratu thought of the boar he would kill, for he knew now he could do it.

Dr. Miller folded his hands behind his head and leaned back. "A good story, quite to my liking," he said. "How did you come up with it?"

"Pieced together from bits of folklore. The natives roar with laughter over the part where Ratu takes advantage of the forest people's superstitions. They even have a ritual dance about it they perform each year."

"Huh. Yeah, it sounds worth dancing about," replied the old biologist, "but what happens next?"

"Oh, generations went by, much as they had before."

"When did the Tarmians arrive here?"

"Not until the second century of the modern era. But it took about another hundred years before they were firmly established, and then they were already being pushed back by barbarians from the north and east." Chris moved his chair out of the shade. The sun was dropping low.

"Ratu's people were here during a relatively warm period," he continued. "The Tarmians happened to come when it was colder. Climate fluctuations cause changes in the environment, but they seem minor compared with civilization, the growth of complex society and cities. Civilization results in real change, to man, the valley, to everything."

"Civilization. I wonder."

Chris grinned. "I can picture you now. If you had lived then you would have had the same sour expression on your face, and you would have constantly complained about how miserable the world is."

"Chris, I'm hurt. You know I love the world. It's wonderful. It's just mankind I have doubts about."

CHAPTER 4

Philosophers

The philosopher stood on the eastern parapet, watching the fishing boats on the lake return to shore in the fading light. He sighed and leaned against the marble column beside him, thinking of the time when he had been more peasant and less courtier, able to do more as he pleased and less as others bade him.

"Well, Pitros," came a mellow voice behind him. "Not at your books today?" A tall man in a purple robe came up beside him. It was Androcles Cratus.

"No, Governor. I think of times past and future." He paused. "It is said we dwell not enough in the present."

"I would agree," replied Cratus. Together they stared silently out at the valley. The provincial governor of the northwest had employed Pitros to tutor his children and be a companion to himself for seven years now. They had learned to understand one another's moods.

A servant came to light the lamps, then went on. The two looked across the lake to where the town Caron lay twinkling in the growing darkness. The island was an excellent spot for the governor's villa. He often stayed there for long periods of time.

"An imperial courier came today," began Cratus, turning to the philosopher. "Northern Gellian is overrun, the third legion put to flight, the civilian population in a panic." He paused for comment, but none came. "So it is in every corner of the empire, even, they say, in Tarma herself."

"Ours is a tumultuous age, my friend. We are fortunate to be here at Tanium."

"I fear destruction will come even to Tanium," whispered the governor.

Pitros thought back to their first meeting, how a worried young Cratus had sought out the thinker from the east to find answers to his problems. They talked five hours that first day and six the next. The day after that Pitros went to live with the nobleman. Cratus lacked confidence then—he had failed in everything he had tried. His army had been routed, his city had revolted, his first book drew sharp criticism from the royalty. Even the tree he planted in his garden at Tarma had died.

Yet this was a noble man, thought the philosopher, studying the young man's nose, the lines on his face, the gentleness of his voice, the soft touch of his hand as it rested on the balustrade. And as his doubts had been worn away in the past few years by sound philosophy, his successes had increased. Each achievement brought with it the seed of another, greater than the one before it. This assignment was just a step away from a councilship at court, and who knew what might lie beyond that?

How would it be to tutor a privy councilor? Or perhaps an emperor, should an old philosopher live longer than is normal? Miserable, probably. Better to be a simple man in a simple village somewhere beyond care.

Pitros shook off his pensiveness. ". . . not relish having to lead against these barbarians," Cratus was saying.

"Yours is a very great duty."

"Yes. My duty."

"The universe is a whole, of which we are but small parts. We must seek out our roles, find and do what we are meant to do."

"And if we balk at the role appointed to us?"

"Then the universe is offended and our place in it becomes twisted. It is like when a carpenter builds a table—if he through forgetfulness, ignorance, or perversity does not include all the legs necessary, the table is unstable and will fall. If a person does not fulfill his duty, there is a void in the universe and the divine order is disrupted."

They walked back into the villa toward the great hall. Pitros continued, "My colleagues in Tarma would not approve of what I just said, of course. Corda, Duros, and the others insist that man is a thing apart from the world, meant only to dominate and subjugate it through the use of mind and muscle, though more of the latter, I fear. They would have us believe we must ever be conquering and destroying other men and nature—a doctrine others in the empire like to hear, true or not.

"But I say there is one whole. We cannot separate mind and body, animal and spirit, any more than we can have life without breath or stars without sky. All things are one thing, in different forms."

The companions reclined on couches in the great hall. The governor summoned servants and ordered food. The servants scurried away, leaving the room empty but for the two friends. Great columns reared up into the shadows, curtains hung between, fires burned in lamps and basins. A breeze blew from the lake, warm and fresh, while the old man talked.

In the middle of the hall, twice the height of a man stood a great blue stone that had been found on the island many years before. Visitors from all over the empire commented on its unusual beauty when they visited the governor, then returned to Tarma full of tales of the distant province's unexpected richness.

Androcles Cratus coughed loudly. A servant came. "Yes, my lord?"

"We've had enough to eat. Have the steward prepare my bed," said the governor, yawning.

"Yes, my Lord."

Cratus stood and said goodnight to the old man. He went toward his apartment. Pitros watched him go, thinking how he had changed. The philosopher smiled and all the wrinkles on his rough old face fell into place. Nodding his head, he fell asleep where he lay in the great hall.

Menton flogged his horse mercilessly as he raced through the night. Behind rode the three men of his guard, hard put to keep up with the procurator. They rushed past field and wood, barn and cottage, toward Tanium and their assignment with the governor. Menton thought of his last meeting with Cratus. Cratus had just lost a thousand septems of the emperor's money at the games and his was the job of collecting.

It certainly was surprising that just ten months later the emperor gave him a governorship. I should have had this from the beginning, thought Menton. I earned it, doing special jobs for the empire, even being errand boy for his majesty. It belongs to me really, not this imperial cousin who has done nothing. He lashed his horse again. This news won't be pleasant for him. Maybe he will die on the front, and since I'll be in Tanium anyway . . .

"Halt and be recognized!" The guard at the ferry shouted.

"Procurator Menton of the imperial staff to see Governor Cratus on urgent business," replied the rider, advancing his horse into the torchlight to show his insignia.

The guard saluted. "Pass, Excellency."

Menton swung his right arm across his breast to return the salute. The riders dismounted and climbed aboard the ferry. The water swirled against the bow and the procurator recalled the richness of the valley, now obscured in darkness. Essential to the salt and amber trade, well located, peaceful and quiet, not to mention easily defensible should the occasion arise.

A rush of autumn air ruffled his crimson cloak, causing him to shiver. If only they could do something about the winters! Only October and already it's colder than Tarma in January, he thought.

The old steward peered sleepily out at the visitors where they stood in the entrance to the great hall. Mud was on their boots, their cloaks were rumpled, their faces were long and haggard, "The governor sleeps, Excellency. You will have to wait until morning," he said firmly.

Ignorant old fool thought Menton. "I have urgent business. That means *now*, Master Steward."

"I'm sorry. It's impossible. I have my orders—he is not to be disturbed." The old man spread his feet apart on the cold marble floor and folded his arms obstinately, looking like an evening thundercloud.

After four days and nights of hard riding, to be stopped by an overly diligent steward not fifty yards from the goal . . . "Very well," said the procurator a little too earnestly, as if it were his idea. "Take me to my quarters, I'll speak with Cratus in the morning. First thing, you understand."

The message would wait, he thought. Perhaps it's better this way anyway, first thing in the morning. It will ruin the boy's whole day.

Menton did not actually see the governor until early afternoon. He steamed into the great hall, past the blue stone and the reflecting pool, to the couch where Cratus lay.

"Good day, my dear Procurator. I am so glad to see you decided to awaken."

"You know perfectly well, Cratus, that I've been up since early this morning and have been seeking audience with you most anxiously. Why have you not wished to see me?"

Ignoring the question, the governor gestured to a chair beside him. "Come, sit here, and deliver your message. Then tell me of Tarma. How is the orange crop?"

Menton sat. This man has grown clever, he thought. "I did not come to discuss oranges. You have not answered my question, but it is no matter. I have a letter from the emperor."

The procurator took a parchment document from his tunic and handed it to Cratus, who fingered the thick red seal. Rich, he thought. They always do things lavishly in Tarma, too lavishly.

"I commend you on your speed and directness. But first let me answer your question. You are pushy and brash, Menton, as always.

It is time you learn patience. If you must learn it in my foyer, then so be it."

Menton's throat burned. He felt the blood rush to his face. This failure, gossiped about all over Tarma, dared to talk so to a trusted servant of the emperor, on a special mission! He clenched his fist out of sight beneath his robe and nodded.

Cratus stared without expression at the letter in his hand. From a side entrance behind a curtain, Pitros entered. He almost winced at the tension in the room, and silently took seat beside the governor.

"According to this . . ."

"Sir," interrupted Menton, casting his eye significantly toward the philosopher.

"It's alright. This is Pitros, my tutor. He is privy to all my affairs, including this one." Menton cleared his throat and continued to look at Pitros. "Now, according to this you are to be my replacement."

The procurator started. He had read the letter before leaving Tarma, carefully resealing it afterwards, and knew it said no such thing. "There must be some misunderstanding."

"No misunderstanding. Don't you think I can read the meaning which is not written? It says I am to assume personal command of the third and fifth legions in the north, while you become my temporary legate and handle the provincial concerns from Tanium. What better way to break in a new governor?"

"I do not know the emperor's intentions. He expressed concern that I gain experience, but as for the governorship . . ." He looked away.

"Oh, don't feel bad, Menton" This will be good for me too, you know. A campaign in the northlands, then what? Return to Tarma. Then senator, prelate, perhaps even councilor."

Menton took stock of this governor in front of him. Blue eyes, short sandy hair, delicate hands; yes, he could be a councilor. A tightness formed in Menton's stomach. "It would seem to be a windfall for both of us, Sir." His voice was too loud.

Cratus stood and walked to the middle of the hall, where he put out his hand and touched the blue stone, tracing a vein through a patch of white, "Assuming, of course, that I return from the campaign."

Menton allowed himself a small inward smile. The emperor's cousin, killed on some lonely outpost by barbarians, leaving behind him a clear road to a soft job with the council for young Menton, newly returned from three or four years of excellent service in an important province. He looked again at the man who shared his thoughts.

"In any case," Cratus continued, "we must get you settled if you are to stay. You didn't bring much. Is your baggage following?"

"Yes, Sir."

"Very well. The steward, Coros, will show you to more comfortable quarters and explain the customs of the house." He clapped his hands and gave orders to the servants who came. Then he turned away from the new legate. "I shall walk in the garden this afternoon. "Will you join me, Pitros?"

"Certainly, my Lord."

Menton watched them go, then followed the steward out the great hall towards his new apartment.

Stands of oak and maple shone red and gold between dark groves of fir and pine on the hillsides beyond the lake. Farther away rose the white peaks of the Tarmian alps, guarded by lesser mountains not yet touched by the frost of winter. To the south lay the heart of the empire, peaceful in the midst of turmoil, or so the foolish were led to believe. Cratus knew the capital to be a ghostly arena filled with struggling shadow-powers, knives at every throat, henchmen at every door.

Relatives of the emperor fought openly to gain influence and powerful posts that might eventually give them the empire itself, while those not fortunate enough to be related bought their places with their souls and with the blood of weaker men. And on all sides tottered the lumbering hulk of the great Tarmian empire, threatened in all its four corners by provincial revolution and war without and civil war within.

Cratus turned to the north. The furthest marches of the alps met those of the Greater Mountains from the east in a gentle concourse of hills and sheltered valleys, like that of Tanium. Wispy clouds faded in the cold air, like worn and withered leaves that had lost their color and whose future held only oblivion. Somewhere beneath those clouds, legions retreated from the barbaric onslaughts surging from the east around the mountains. There he must lead and inspire his men to face death boldly.

"Pitros," he asked, "where would you be if Tarma did not exist and had not taken you from your homeland to make a tutor of you?"

The old man thought a moment. He replied, "My father was a teacher and an artist. I imagine I would have done what he did, and probably would have died in some futile war against some other empire, as he did."

"Yes, some other empire. Have you ever wondered what it is that makes men build such monstrosities?"

"I have. It seems to be inherent in the nature of things that some men seek dominion, others do not. And when those who desire power actually gain it, they immediately begin to abuse it. I do not think there is any other explanation." The philosopher fell silent.

"I've grown to love Tanium, Pitros. It is hard to leave."

"You will come again, my Lord."

"No, I think not. Perhaps I shall pass through, but I do not believe I shall ever live here again. I regret that. This place has a timelessness about it. It seems somehow greater than the ordinary . . ." He shrugged his shoulders.

"Tanium does have a remarkable quality about it, Androcles. I think 'restful' is the word, though that is inadequate."

"Yes, of course." The governor stared at the lake again. As he watched, a fleet of fishing boats moved slowly from shore, their captains having returned from the noon meal and rest, ready to work their nets again. The boats moved gracefully, like gulls that have found a warm air current and glide from place to place above a troubled sea.

"How long do you expect the war in the north to continue?" asked Pitros.

Cratus folded his arms. "Oh, this campaign shouldn't be more than a year or a year and a half. The war? I do not think the war will ever be over, unless in a way not to our liking."

"You are gloomy today. But come, we were going to the garden." The old man led the governor past the parapet, down a long corridor, through a vine-covered archway. The temperature was noticeably higher in the enclosure. It was heated by steam to keep the delicate plants alive.

Red and white roses still bloomed there, as well as asphodel, daphnia, and geraniums; sweet fragrances rose from the basil, marjoram, and savory; as they walked their feet broke tiny sprouts of thyme where it grew in the cracks of the pavement, adding that scent to the air. All mingled soothingly, like a delicious stew by an expert chef.

The two companions sat on a bench between a grape vine and a fig tree and thought of the changes in their lives.

The philosopher watched the governor and his party board the little ferry that would take them to shore, to their waiting horses. They were travelling light—a handful of aides, a couple servants, a dozen guards—but the little boat rode low in the water under the weight, moving sluggishly into the lake.

Menton stood beside the old man. "Do you plan to join Cratus's family in Tarma?"

"The other way around, I am leaving for Tarma next week; they will join me." Pitros noted the other's haughty face. He thought, though I will miss this valley as no other place since childhood, I am glad to leave you behind.

"It is well. See that nothing is left behind of their property, will you? I won't be responsible if something is broken or lost." The new legate threw a final glance at the ferry and vanished into the villa.

It was early. The rays of sun slanted down from the eastern sky into the valley, changing the blue haze to brilliant white, firing the fall colors, deepening the greens that stood out here and there in the forest.

The water glistened, and over it all hung a cloud of anticipation. Pitros remained where he stood, pulling at his white beard.

"Another good story, Chris. Also pieced together from old lore?" asked the biologist.

"I added my own details, of course, but the history for this period is much more complete than earlier times."

"What happened to them? To Cratus and the rest?"

"Well, we don't know much about Pitros. He was not a writer. But Cratus was successful in his northern campaign. He is famous in Tarmian history for his wonderful book of philosophy, *Meditations on the Good, the True, and the Beautiful*. Didn't you have to read it in school?"

The old biologist chuckled, "I remember the title, but no, once I had completed the required courses it was all science and math for me. And detective novels." He glanced around again at the abundant vegetation of the valley. "I will put it on my list for when I retire."

"After that campaign Cratus went back to Tarma. Eventually became a senator."

"What about the other guy?"

"Menton? He is most remembered for the savagery with which he put down the native rebellion here in Tanium. The emperor rewarded him with a councilship, but later had him executed for treason. His ambition ran ahead of his skill."

Dr. Miller scratched his chin. "That seems somehow predictable."

They sat a while in silence.

"And then? What happened after that?" he asked.

CHAPTER 5

The Mercenary

The stranger came in, stamping his feet and brushing the snow from his coat and hat. He closed the heavy wood door behind him. He was tall with long brown hair and beard and deep-set eyes flecked with green. He removed his fur coat, exposing a short fighting sword that had seen much use.

"Thank you," he said smoothly.

"No thanks necessary," replied Sart. "No one should stay out on a night like this. Besides, you invited yourself, as I recall."

"I'd heard you are a good man, and generous."

"There are many lies in the land," said Sart.

While the old man stoked the fire and put a pot of water over it the stranger spread his coat on a bench and made himself comfortable by the big wood table that filled one end of the room. Sart went into the pantry and brought out coarse bread, goat cheese, and a small flagon of wine. "Cold and simple fare, but it'll have to do tonight. You can have hot tea when it's ready. Then you'll tell me who you are and what your business in Kar-un might be." He sat in a chair nearby and eyed his visitor.

"My name is Stephen Saryan," the stranger said when he had finished, "and I came here to meet you."

Sart showed his surprise. "Me? What would a strong young man like you want with an old farmer?"

"You were not always a farmer."

The old man waited to reply. "No, not always. But it's ten years since I lifted a brick. If you want something built, you'll just have to go elsewhere." The fire sputtered and flared, casting strange shadows on the gloomy cottage's floor and walls.

The stranger took a sip of tea, "Why did you retire?"

"Why does anyone retire? I was tired of it. I like my life as it is now."

"I see. What was your last job?"

Sart looked at his guest keenly, He noted a white scar above his left jaw, the kind left by a sword. What did he want? "Repair work at the Burg. Why?"

"I am interested in your experience. What do . . ."

"Just a moment," interrupted Sart. "You come in here asking a lot of questions like a constable. I don't even know who you are." He felt his fingers tremble with apprehension.

"I gave you my name," said the stranger.

"And what should that tell me?"

Saryan searched the old man's face. He raised his right hand, pulled at his short beard. "I will tell you more if first you say—are you loyal to Baron Reichenhall?"

Sart's mouth twitched as he lied, "Of course." Then added ironically, "As loyal as any other citizen of the barony."

"And what of Duke Druin?"

Did this stranger want to trap him? He spoke slowly. "The duke is revered by all who have had dealings with him and remember his justice. Nevertheless, I am of Reichenhall."

Saryan had caught the flicker in Sart's eyes; he leaned across the table.

"I am a servant of the duke," he whispered, "and require your loyalty and silence. Will you give this?"

The old man sighed and asked, "Why should I believe you?"

Saryan took a pendant from beneath his tunic and held it up for the man to see. On it was the polished image of a man on horseback, spear in hand, a turquoise star shining over the left shoulder, "Have you known any but a duke's man to wear one of these?"

Sart rubbed his brow. He had not seen such a pendant since coming to his farm. "You have my word."

"And what of your loyalty to the baron?"

The old man spat on the floor. "I am as loyal to him as he is to the people. I rejoice at his death."

Both smiled grimly and huddled together. "Tell me all you can about the Burg, every detail, especially the guns. Could you draw a map, a diagram?"

The fire hissed and burned low. Outside, the wind whistled, piling drifts of snow wherever it could in the pale light of the moon. When morning came the landscape was harsh white in the early winter sun. Kar-un and Newtown on the far side of the lake stood out like dirty patches on a clean tablecloth, while before them stretched the water, its deep darkness broken only by the rocky island in the center. On the island was Burg Reichenhall, an enormous black edifice with pastel spires etched in frosty lace. It was built upon the ruins of other ancient fortresses right back to before the Tarmians.

Stephen Saryan and Sart Kaladson looked out at the scene and marveled at the day's brilliance. White smoke rose from a hundred chimneys to join the frozen mist that hung in patches above the valley.

"Now we must part, friend. I speak for the duke when I say thank you."

Sart grasped the young man's hand. "If I were your age I would offer more. Godspeed."

Saryan pulled his hat down tight around his ears. The snow crunched beneath his feet as he walked quickly down the road that led through Kar-un to the landing where he could board the island ferry.

The old man looked after him and said to himself, "If he lives, he may do much good. If not, it will not matter to me. My life will not change." He went back into his house and closed the door behind him.

"So, you are a soldier of fortune and wish to join my personal guard, eh?" Baron Reichenhall snarled, his jowls jiggling. He belched and put down the turkey bone he had been gnawing. "You there," he bellowed at a nearby page. "Take this away!"

The baron leaned back in his chair and pulled at the purple tunic draped over his massive body, leaving spots with his greasy fingers. He stared at the young man who had sought audience with him so early in the morning. "Well Master Saryan, tell me about yourself. Why should I desire your service?"

"I am an experienced man-at-arms, Sire, with knowledge of every modern weapon and of both the Tarmian and Chivalric codes. I have served three masters since the beginning of my career, Count Justin of Troyka, Count Leopold of Tarma, and His Majesty, the King of Monikeea."

He pulled a letter from his breast pocket and handed it to the baron. "Here is a letter of recommendation."

"You were with the late king? How did you find the southern climes?"

"Hot," replied Saryan.

The baron snorted and said, "And what of those barbarian fanatics? Are they as hot as their desert?"

"They are excellent fighters, Excellency."

"I imagine they are," laughed Reichenhall. "They killed your king and routed your army. Tell me, have you ever had command?"

"I captained a company of bowmen for the king."

"A captain, no less. We've no place for another captain at the moment." He turned to a soldier who stood nearby. "If you are as good as you claim, Saryan, you will be trained as lieutenant of the castle guard. But first we must see if you can fight." He motioned to the soldier, who drew his sword and advanced.

Saryan feinted into the middle of the great hall. A dozen spectators—ladies, guards, advisors—stood along each wall. He grabbed a chair from among them and thrust it onto the point of his attacker's blade, then disarmed him in one swift motion. His petard at the soldier's throat, Saryan looked at the Baron. The audience murmured in wonder.

"Well done, Lieutenant Saryan. An admirable job, swift and to the point." He laughed at his pun and added, "Too swift for entertainment purposes, unfortunately. You are hired." He picked a piece of meat from between his teeth, then gestured to another man standing by. "This is Milcar, your captain. He will show you to your quarters."

Reichenhall stood and approached his new officer. He put out his hand, shook Saryan's, then unexpectedly pulled Saryan to him. Saryan smelled the man's sweet wine breath as the baron whispered gutturally, "One other thing, my dear Lieutenant. I am Valya Reichenhall. My family has held this land for four centuries, since first we came from the north, and I demand the strictest obedience from my men in all things. If ever I see a hint of cowardice or betrayal from you, I will personally rip your heart from your chest and feed it to my herdsman's dogs."

He pushed Saryan from him, then watched him bow submissively and leave with Milcar before returning to his padded chair. "That should keep him in line," he said quietly. "For now."

The baron had learned long ago always to back up threats with object lessons, things even a fool can understand. The best lessons are ones that work on someone's weakness. And everyone has weakness, even a captain of the Monikeean king.

He looked around at the people in the hall. All pieces on a great game board waiting to be moved and manipulated. And I, thought Valya, I am the man to make the rules and do the moving.

Suddenly a heavily cloaked yeoman burst in through the great double doors at the far end of the hall. He ran its length, bending low as he approached the dais where sat the baron. He coughed hoarsely. "Excellency!"

"Your message, Tolgar."

"It is as you thought, Excellency," whispered the messenger. "They attempt an inland route by the Foothills Road. They stopped at Krammer Landing, unloaded, and continued from there. And Sire, a ducal guard accompanies them." The man's lips were touched with blue, and his breath came in gasps."

"A ducal guard, you say? Does your commander think he can take them?"

"Yes, my Lord."

"And has he taken steps to carry out my orders in that regard?"

"Yes, my Lord."

"Very good, Tolgar. Page, escort this faithful soldier to a place where he can rest and recover from his journey." He clapped his hands.

But Tolgar didn't move. "Sire," he said, "Captain Smit requires reinforcements as soon as possible if he is to carry out the second part of your instructions. The duke's men were not expected and make the whole operation more difficult."

"Reinforcements?" The baron's face darkened. "I'll consider it, Tolgar. And you will be with him as soon as you recover from your journey."

Valya Reichenhall watched the man go. He noted how he already seemed much better than when he arrived, but still shivered in the great hall, which was hardly warmer than outside, though sheltered from the wind. He stood up from the dais, pulled his cloak around his shoulders, and stepped down to where a fire burned on a large open hearth. The smoke curled up in great clouds to the rafters above and hid among the shadows, sometimes briefly reappearing if a cross breeze happened into the upper reaches.

Valya heard murmuring among the dozen or so hangers-on in the court. Not all had known of the operation against the landing, and now they were wondering if their position in the baron's favor was as secure as they had thought. The baron smiled. It could not have worked out better if I had planned it, he thought. Of course, these are all loyal, and except for the most crucial details they know all that is done and decided. Still, they are pawns, all of them.

A hawk-faced man with grey-streaked hair and shoulders that drooped a little approached the baron and put his wrinkled hands over the fire. "Some of your councilors worry that you did not tell them of your intentions, my Lord," he said in a low voice.

"Let them worry. It will keep them careful." This one is no pawn, thought Reichenhall. A rook perhaps, but no pawn.

"And do you intend to destroy Krammer Landing completely?"

"What do you think, Squire Dedham? Would I do anything halfway?" His lips curled in a fierce snarl, showing his teeth.

"No, Sire, certainly not. Yet there is something about the whole affair which bothers me. I recall that your father once told me, 'When maneuvering for position, never over-extend your forces. Better to be successful in a small thing than fail attempting a big one.'"

Valya looked at his aged councilor. "Yes, Squire, I recall my father said many things. I also recall that he died young, leaving a foolish man as regent and a vacant spot in the family hall." He gestured toward where a framework on the floor betrayed the absence of some large object. "That blue stone was the backdrop for the christening of the Barons of Reichenhall since the beginning of our modern civilization, put there as a token of trust by the last great Tarmian emperor, but my father let it be taken away to some unknown land, not to mention the other riches we once had. No, I will not soon forget those things."

The squire remained silent. Valya glanced past him. "Ah, the baroness comes." From a private entrance behind the dais a tall, slender woman approached. Her long blond hair was caught up in loose clusters on her head, and her gown rustled and swished like leaves of the forest.

"Good morning, my dear; I trust you slept well." said the baron, returning to his chair.

"Very well, my lord, though it did grow quite cold, did it not?" Her blue eyes swept the hall, taking in the courtiers and advisors, registering the concerned looks on many faces. "Am I disturbing an important audience?" she asked.

"Of course not, Lady Arla," replied the baron. "We have merely been discussing steps we may take—and are taking—to ensure the salt and amber revenues."

"I see. What are those steps, may I ask?"

Valya glanced quickly at his consort. He had always felt a bit distrustful of this woman. But it was an important alliance, one which would assure a future even if there were disaster in the barony. "I have moved against the smugglers, my dear. They thought to wind around the lake, thus avoiding the payment of our tax at Wood Village, where Great River empties into the lake. When we are finished with this shipment, we shall take further action to prevent a repeat of such dishonesty."

"I see. And what shall that be, my Lord?"

This really does not concern her, thought the baron. "We will destroy Krammer Landing, where the smugglers' road begins. If necessary, we will leave a garrison, but I don't think that will be required."

Arla was silent. She reflected on her years with the baron. Always there were thieves to be attacked, always some war or rebellion to be dealt with, and always the conflicts were over such little matters. She noticed Valya tugging at his shirt, trying to make it cover his bulk. And always Valya grew fatter, she thought. Each year it was the same: battle, victory, celebration. And each celebration seemed to add several pounds to the baron's frame. She sighed. Marriages of state could not take into account such things, yet at times her personal feelings prevailed. She said, "My Lord, I won't stay to bother you. I'll be in my apartments."

"Very well, my dear. I shall join you for dinner." He felt relieved to see her go. Now to the matter of reinforcements. "Toring," he said. A dark little man detached himself from the group of retainers that had entered a few moments before. "What is the status of the duke's troops?"

Toring wet his lips. "Aside from the men at Krammer Landing and with the salt shipment from the south, all his soldiers are garrisoned at Kar-point and Druinberg, Sire."

"There is no chance of an attack from him on Kar-un or Newtown, then?"

"There would not seem to be, Sire."

"And the Barons Feldschmidt and Wahrham?"

"Neither is in a position to harm us at the present time, my Lord."

Valya smiled a gloating smile and fingered his sparse black beard. "Good! I want fifty men-at-arms and thirty bowmen ready to march to Captain Smit at Krammer Landing by this afternoon. And have that new man—Saryan—go with the archers. I want to be told how well he performs. Do you understand?"

"Yes, my Lord."

Baron Reichenhall looked at his court, the retainers and advisors, the guards along the wall, the paintings hung here and there. Pawns and rooks, he thought, all to be moved about like the paintings on the wall, according to my fancy. And in the field, I have more of them, and a queen here at home. All to be manipulated at my will. So starts another game, with the last one not quite finished.

CHAPTER 6

The Lady

Smit's troops rendezvoused with the reinforcements shortly before noon, about three miles below Krammer Landing. They were tired after the long march and the battle the day before, but the sight of fresh men heartened and encouraged them, doubling their ranks despite the loss of those killed and those who were sent with the booty to Wood Village.

The men huddled around small fires, trying to keep warm in the icy forest, hoping no smoke would be spotted at the landing. Captain Smit and his lieutenant met with Commander Tolg and Saryan beneath two large fir trees.

"This is Stephen Saryan, the baron's new lieutenant of the guard. He's leading the archers I brought," said Tolg, signaling to Smit that Saryan was not to be completely trusted, not yet.

"Your brother, Tolgar, mentioned you were bringing a new one when he came to tell of our rendezvous. Welcome to the baron's service, Lieutenant." A smile came smartly to Smit's face, yellow teeth showing in the space between black beard and black moustache.

Saryan saw the deceit in the captain's eyes. "Thank you, Sir." Here is a key man, he thought. He stamped his feet on the frozen ground.

"Now to plan the attack," said the captain, his voice as harsh as the air around them. "They will no doubt have had word of our victory against the salt shipment and will be prepared for us. They won't know that we are so many, however. We may try to surround the landing. If we can force a surrender, that would be best—take a few prisoners and burn a few houses, then return to Kar-un."

"The baron mentioned destroying the landing," said Saryan.

Smit raised his eyebrows. "That is just talk, for show, as is this attack. To scare the troublemakers. We need the landing, and we need the people to work."

"And the duke's men?"

"You heard about that, too? The ducal guard already left, heading south, so we needn't worry about getting them involved."

He pulled a parchment map from his pocket and showed how the landing was set against the river in a place where the water grew sluggish. They talked for about an hour, then broke camp and made their way along the river toward their goal. It was early afternoon before they dispersed according to plan around Krammer Landing. Saryan and his bowmen were concealed in the trees at the brow of a hill overlooking the spot. On their left rolled Great River on its way to the lake in the southwest, now barely visible as a twinkling patch of dark blue amid the white hills which stretched away in all directions.

Smit's men were on the other side of the landing, Tolg's yeomen on the right. Tolgar, the messenger, had been assigned to Saryan's troop. He approached him now and said, "All is ready, Lieutenant Saryan.

"Good," came the reply. "Smit will initiate the attack. We will follow."

Tolgar watched his commander carefully. A good soldier, this. He was experienced; you could tell by the easy way he crouched behind the tree and fitted shaft to string—with an oiled ease, as if on the practice field. But he remembered Smit's words to him: "Watch Saryan. Stay with him. If there is any reluctance, any sign of disobedience or treachery, dispatch him immediately and assume command." Nothing could have been plainer.

"You needn't worry about that," said Saryan.

"Worry about what, Sir?" asked Tolgar, surprised.

"About having to kill me. I won't betray our baron."

"I have no doubt of that, Sir."

Saryan turned to him and smiled. "Maybe not, but your brother does. We may have a little wait. Tell me about yourself. Have you always been a soldier for the baron?"

Tolgar hesitated. "No, Sir. Tolg and I had a farm in Newtown, but the house burned down. It was then that the war with Baron Wahrham broke out and he and I were in the levy. We stayed on after, as there wasn't much to go home to." He bit his lip and his dark eyes seemed to turn inward a moment. Then he said, "It's a good enough life, I reckon. We don't want for anything."

"How about pay. Is the baron good for that?"

"Yes, Sir." He grinned. "Pay's good, and the spoils. There's traffic enough through the valley, so we do real fine. And it'll be even better when we have a garrison at the landing and have closed the road that leads around this end of the lake to Druinberg. Nothing can go past Wood Village without coming under the guns of Burg Reichenhall,"

Saryan smiled at his new friend. "Are the guns as big as they say? I've not had a chance to see them."

"Big? Why, they're huge! The baron had them specially made, shipped all the way from Tarma. Before that, most of the traders got by without paying a cent—slim enough pickings, let me tell you. Especially after the war when everything had drained the country so. But with these three guns things have been getting better and better."

Suddenly there came a shout from the little town below. Smit's men charged from their cover, a shower of arrows going before them. Men rushed to the low wood and earth walls of the town to return fire. Someone rang a bell; others ran from their homes, confused and afraid. Tolg advanced on the west. Saryan waited until the town walls immediately below were empty, all the defenders having gone to the other side. Then he waved at the archers behind him. Arrows rained on the town some fifty yards distant. He gave the order to charge.

The defenders were indeed surprised by the number of their attackers. The battle was brief. Flames from several houses roared into the air and streamlets of melted snow ran into the ground. The wounded were gathered into a low storage building by the landing, but the men strewn on the ground nearby were beyond help. Tolg's yeomen collected the bodies for burial.

"A fine victory," said Smit, eyes gleaming.

"We lost more than we should have," Tolg muttered. "It was a black day."

They made camp. Tomorrow would see them back in the garrison at Kar-un. They were happy at the thought, but this night would be cold and cheerless in the few buildings spared destruction. Saryan looked at the thick cloud layer that rolled in through the gap between the mountains, threatening fresh snow before dark. Even as he looked, the first few flakes fell on the chilly valley.

Smit would later report to the baron about Saryan's conduct. "But did he kill anyone?" he was asked.

"I did not see that myself, Sire, but he led his archers well. Tolgar spoke highly of him."

"Hmm."

"The yeoman did most of the fighting. They surrendered quickly; I think they did not expect us to attack in such cold weather or to have so many soldiers."

"Very well," replied the baron. He smiled. "I cannot argue with victory."

Squire Dedham, don't you think Master Saryan has a nice head?" asked Lady Arla, laughing.

"Quite, my Lady. An excellent subject." The squire's grey beard pressed to a point when he smiled.

"Do you hear that, Master Saryan? The good squire agrees with me. I shall paint your portrait whether you like it or not." She walked to where he stood in the middle of her studio and pulled at his tunic. "But I will not tolerate wrinkles in the uniform. Such a pretty uniform the guard has. And your sword must be drawn, the point touching your right foot."

The two chamber maids standing near the door tittered and whispered to each other. Saryan was only mildly perturbed.

"My Lady, I must protest," he said. "My duties won't permit me to be away from my post for long . . ."

"Hush! I won't hear a word of it," returned Arla. "I am going to paint your portrait even if I have to fetch Valya and have him order you to stand still for it." She pursed her lips. "In the months you've been with us you've yet to tell anyone about your homeland. We are all very eager to hear your story, Master Saryan. So. It is settled."

The studio was large and brightly lit, a sharp contrast to the rest of the castle. Great double windows, the glass faintly purple, let in the late winter sunshine. At one end of the room stood three looms with partly finished projects still on them. Nearby were drawers full of yarn, hooks, sweaters, and other crafts and implements of the lady and her maids. The south end of the room was entirely devoted to Arla's painting with several easels and canvases. And everywhere was color—greens, blues, reds, and yellows, glistening like a giant rainbow.

Squire Dedham excused himself while one of the maids found an empty canvas and put it on the waiting easel. Said Lady Arla, "You know, Master Saryan, you are most fortunate. At the court of my father, I am known as an excellent artist."

"I am fortunate in many ways, my Lady."

"Oh?"

"It is rare that a simple soldier may remain so long in such a wonderful room, in the company of such a charming lady."

"What?" She feigned astonishment. "You are gallant as well as pretty. I am flattered, Master Saryan."

Saryan looked at the artist and resigned himself to his duty. He had learned much in the past weeks about the ways of the castle, the intrigues of court, the moods and thoughts of the baron. Yet here was one unknown element—Lady Arla. The distaste she felt for the baron was obvious to anyone with eyes to see, but her loyalty was unquestioned. She seemed above the baron, beyond the interests of a petty barony, greater than the everyday, yet somehow near the center of it.

"Tell me of your father and his court, my Lady," he asked.

Arla looked at him in surprise. "I asked you about your homeland, not the other way around. But since you ask . . ." She put down the charcoal with which she had been sketching. "My father is noble, courtly, honest, and kind in all he does, even the dangerous things. I assume you are familiar with his military successes?"

"Of course."

"Those are a necessary part of life, I suppose, but soldiering is not who he really is. The court is light and gay—it doesn't grow so abominably cold there as here. In fact, I dare say spring flowers are already in bloom. Father has a much larger court than the baron. Naturally, he conducts a considerable amount of business and has vast properties. As chief of the Southlands Council he is constantly active and has an interest in everything there is.

"But what of you, Master Saryan?" She picked up the charcoal again and made sweeping marks on the paper that was laid over the canvas.

"I was born in Troyka, Madam. My father was the captain of the count's guard. I was raised to arms, entered my first combat at the age of fifteen . . ."

"Such a mechanical recitation! You sound as though you are giving me a memorized speech, as if applying for a job. I want to know about your people, how you lived in Troyka, not how qualified you are to be lieutenant of the guard."

He felt a warmth in his heart. Here was a person interested in life, not just in armies and maneuvers and intrigues. Her eyes sparkled a far-away blue and the smile on her lips made him think, *if such souls are spies, we should all have secrets.*

"My people are simple people," he began. "We served the count loyally, and he was our friend as well as our master. He treated our family as his own. Once, in battle, he risked his own life to draw my wounded father from the field. He always cared for us, and we loved him.

"But it was not to remain forever so. The old count died, and his son was not kind. He exiled my father for some foolish, trumped-up charge. I followed, only to find he had fallen ill and died on the road. It was then I set out to find a new master like the old count."

Saryan thought of his meeting Duke Druin and how their friendship had flourished in the hot lands of the south while serving the king. It would be imprudent to tell that part of the story.

"And have you found such a master?" asked the baroness.

"No," he lied.

"What of our dear baron?" asked Arla.

"The baron is a good master, but I've not been in his service long enough to know him well."

Their eyes met briefly and reflected kindred experiences, similar feelings. Arla looked down. "Yours is a sad story, Master Saryan. I thank you for sharing it."

She put down the charcoal. "We've done enough for one day. We will do more tomorrow."

Arla extended her hand and Saryan kissed it. He felt it tremble ever so slightly in his own sure grip. "Thank you for your patience, Master Saryan.

"It is I who am grateful, my Lady," he replied.

He is not all he seems, she thought as he left. Or perhaps he is more.

CHAPTER 7

Chess Players

A stealthy figure moved from shadow to shadow in the pale moonlight, across the castle courtyard toward the stairway that led to the baron's apartments. A drowsy guard nearby pulled the edge of his cloak more tightly around him as a biting wind breathed over the lake. He did not see the man in the courtyard. The man reached the door, opened it, closed it, climbed silently up the stairs.

Justice, thought Squire Dedham. This is in the name of justice. Your just reward for the years of misrule and terror you've inflicted on a helpless countryside. Always a war or a feud. And if there isn't one going on you make one by attacking some harmless trader who, by accident of geography, is forced to enter your abominable precincts.

Dedham felt his cheeks tingle, felt the cold stone walls become warmer as he approached the apartments, felt the round pommel of his gold dagger.

Squire, you call me. Can a person be squire when all his peasants are dead or in the army? Is a squire one who owns unworked land while the farmers go fight somewhere or steal from passers-by? You've taken from me my claim to title, what little of it there was.

Justice, thought Dedham, for a fat pig who murders everything it sees and thinks itself a man for having a bigger mire than anyone else. A wave of nausea came over him as he thought of the villain that lay in bed just a few feet away on the other side of the thick wooden door he now faced, He thought of the pool of blood that would surround the beast as it died. Drawing his dagger from its gem-encrusted sheath, Dedham reached for the door handle.

"Don't do it," came a harsh whisper from behind him. A hand gripped him by the shoulder. Dedham whirled around to face his discoverer.

It was Saryan.

"Don't do it, I say. You'll do more harm than good." Saryan took the blade from the old man.

"He's a murderer, Saryan. He deserves to die," returned Dedham, his voice deep and tremulous.

"As lieutenant of the guard I should kill you where you stand," said Saryan. He studied the old squire. "But you are a good man, and a useful one. Leave here immediately, and don't try it again. You will gain your life."

"No," said Dedham, his eyes ablaze. "I am in your power. I have failed in my duty. Carry out yours."

"You're a fool, Squire. Don't you realize what would have happened if you had killed him? He has no children, Dedham. No children." Saryan shook the man by his tunic. "If he died now Smit would take the barony by force. If you think Reichenhall is cruel, Smit would be ten times worse. This country would never be the same."

The truth of what Saryan said struck the squire like a blow. He reeled back, eyes wide. "Of course," he whispered. "How could I have been so blind?"

Saryan returned his dagger. "Now get out of here while the guard sleeps. Leave the baron alone."

Squire Dedham mumbled his thanks then stumbled back down the passageway to the stairs beyond. Saryan thought, I must act soon. The water is boiling, and I can't let the situation get out of hand before I finish.

He glanced at the door to the baron's apartment, turned, and moved quietly along the dimly lit corridor toward his own quarters near the guard tower.

It was one of those rare late winter days that presage the coming spring. Snow lay here and there on the shore and in shaded places around the castle, but the sun shone bright, the sky was clear, and a warm breeze blew. One of the castle craftsmen took his work into the courtyard to enjoy the weather. He was a wood carver, preparing a set of four bedposts for the baron, each of which would have on it a seasonal scene.

Each chip was carefully cut from the remaining block as the old man leaned over the wood, humming softly to himself, and occasionally grunting at a tough spot or a knot. His hair was white as the snow so recently melted. From beneath bushy brows peered mellow grey eyes that examined each new stroke in the light of many years, comparing it with past work as a test of its quality.

Chip, chip; slice, slice; gradually the scenes took shape. Spring was a naked wood nymph hiding behind young willow shoots by a rushing stream. Summer was a hunter with drawn bow and jaunty hat chasing a hart with saliva pouring from its mouth. Autumn was a fat man with a pipe in his mouth, fresh grapes, corn, and grain in his hands. Winter was an old man with a long beard, huddled before a fire, his children gathered around to hear a tale of ancient days and empire.

And in the lower right-hand corner of each was a tiny double triangle, a mark indicating to those who cared that these carvings were not done by any ordinary carver in some out-of-the-way village, but by a master of the art, one who lived and breathed his craft and could challenge the best to surpass his excellence.

Stephen Saryan leaned against a pillar on the balcony that overlooked the courtyard and watched the man below. Beyond the castle walls the lake shone glinting blue, its surface agitated gently by the wind. How alike they are, he mused—the old carver and the lake—both timeless as earth and fire, going on about their business, hardly touched by the dreams and aspirations of those who presume to be great.

"Well, Master Saryan," said Lady Arla as she approached him. "Enjoying our beautiful spring weather?" She thought how handsome he was, there in the sunlight.

"It is a nice day, my Lady", said Saryan. The carver continued chip, chip in the courtyard below.

They were silent for a few moments. She wondered what he was going to say, or if he was going to say anything at all. What a stolid man he seems, she thought. His jaw suggests strength and his brow intelligence.

"I hope to begin painting today," she said. "Enough of sketches, I think."

"That's good, my Lady." He smiled, suspecting her thoughts. Then he looked again at the old man and was caught up in the workings of his own mind.

"I saw Squire Dedham today. He was frightfully pale and wouldn't say a word. I do hope he isn't ill."

"Not ill," he said.

"Oh? You know something of the matter then?"

Saryan turned to face her. "A little. The good squire is worried about some personal matters. Nothing too important, I believe. At any rate, nothing we can help with."

Slice, slice went the carver's blade below them.

"He certainly was agitated about it, whatever it is," said Arla in reply. She looked at the old man at work and she felt a chill. "Have you ever felt like a helpless block of wood, Master Saryan, and been afraid as the knife comes ever closer?"

They both watched a while longer in silence before he replied. "If you are ready, my Lady, perhaps we can finish the portrait before spring is here in full." They turned toward her studio and were joined by her maids.

On the far side of the court Smit stepped from the shadows and scowled at the two as they left the balcony. Beside him stood Valya Reichenhall, stroking his beard thoughtfully. "Perhaps you are right," he rumbled.

"The lieutenant seems a more than willing subject for your lady's painting, Sire," said Smit.

"Yes."

Valya was annoyed at his captain's disturbing him with rumors about Arla. It is obvious Smit is jealous. That's his problem, he thought. As far as Lady Arla is concerned there is nothing to worry about. She is loyal, if not to me then to her father, and that precludes injuring me either physically or politically.

Saryan is still in doubt, however. He did well enough at Krammer Landing, and there has been nothing to complain about in his service here, but his background is simply too vague. What if he's an agent? And if he's an agent, why has Lady Arla taken such a liking to him? Valya shook his head in disgust. Oh, the whole thing's because Smit's jealous, he decided.

"Alright, Smit, keep an eye on him. Report anything suspicious. And Smit, keep an eye on yourself as well." Valya glared at his captain and stalked across the courtyard past the woodcarver toward the kitchens. All this nonsense had made him hungry. He hoped the baker would have a fresh hot loaf or two.

The woodcarver noticed nothing, not even Smit, who studied him for several minutes more before climbing the balcony steps. He went on with his cutting, slowly and meticulously, as befitted one so expert in his art.

Saryan moved as silently as possible along the narrow passage that led to the east tower. The walls were damp and dark. The little scuffling sounds he made were thought by the guards on the other side of the walls to be rats, scurrying to their nests with stolen morsels from the dining halls below. This was one of those faint lines leading from nowhere to nothing that Sart had drawn on the map he made for Saryan three months before. He touched both walls with his hands, felt moisture running down them, noticed that it had increased. The darkness was almost tangible. It seemed to press on Saryan from all sides, smothering him. He sighed a deep sigh.

At last, he felt a tiny crack under his right palm. He scratched along it, found the outline of a small door about three feet tall. On the side hung a lever. He pushed and it creaked faintly. A sliver of light appeared around the door. No one was in the artillery room, but two torches blazed on the wall, struggling to brighten this place of evil reputation.

Saryan stepped into the middle of the room and stared at the huge guns that were aimed at the lake. They stood taller than he, their great bronze castings bound together with layers of planks tied with wire. Bolted to the floor, they were barely movable but for the slack that had been allowed for recoil.

Accurate aiming was impossible. But accuracy was rarely needed, for when a poor ship's captain saw the cloud of smoke from the tower, heard the thunder, and felt the jostling of the waves, he almost invariably surrendered to the baron's launches coming at him from Wood Village.

A cold draft from the open gun bays reminded Saryan of his task. He rushed from gun to gun, taking the kegs of blasting powder that stood under the breaches where the cannons were bolted down and jamming them more tightly beneath the guns. In each keg he put the end of a long fuse cut from the supply hanging on the wall. All the while he worked, he thought of the fire and destruction the black dust would cause, how the wood would burn, the stones would crack, and the guns would be bent and twisted beyond repair.

Finally, the lake passage would be free again. Cargoes could be shipped the easiest way and no more than one in ten would be taxed by the barons of Reichenhall. But Saryan knew his effort would ultimately be in vain. New weapons would be shipped in from Tarma and other places where such things were used, maybe even small ones that could be used by two or three men in hand-to-hand fighting. What would become of the world when that day came? Would there even be a reason to fight? Saryan shook his head and took a torch from the wall. Today is this day, and the job is this one, he thought. There will be time enough to worry about tomorrow.

He held the flame to each fuse until it flared, then went to the next. As the third fuse caught, there was a scraping sound behind him. Saryan whirled to see Captain Smit pull himself into the room.

"So," said Smit grinning evilly, "the traitor shows himself at last. And what do you think you're doing here?"

Saryan stood stunned.

"Perhaps you've come to inspect the artillery. But why would you need to come after midnight? Come now, can't you think fast enough to give me an answer?" He moved toward Saryan, drawing his sword. "I should call the guards and have them kill you, but I would rather have the pleasure myself. It will take at least five minutes for those fuses to burn—time enough to escape, time enough to be entertained."

Saryan transferred the torch to his left hand, drew his sword, and stepped back before his attacker. Smit lunged, parried, jumped away. It would not be an easy fight, Saryan knew. This was no simple soldier, no tired caravan trooper; Smit was an expert killer, feared by all for his great skill and even greater bloodlust.

Saryan threw the torch in the captain's face, followed it with a drive to the man's mid-section, turned, and jumped to the left.

"A good move," said Smit. "But now you have no more torches." Smit lunged again and Saryan feinted, this time to the right. There was a sudden coldness in his side, then a burning sensation. He put his hand to the spot and glanced at the sticky red that oozed between his fingers.

"Well, traitors bleed, too. It is nice to know."

Saryan glanced at the fuses. They burned low already. Smit lunged again.

He talks too much, thought Saryan. He's not paying close enough attention to the fuses. He's easily distracted, and that's a fault. And any fault can be used, if only there is time.

Saryan parried and gave way toward the door that led to the guard room some yards distant. With his left hand he found the latch, fumbled with it, and pushed the door until it opened. The two fought into the vaulted corridor beyond.

"Afraid of the fire, Saryan?" Smit grinned.

The fool! He hasn't been watching. His timing is off. Saryan looked past Smit as the first fuse sputtered into the powder and a ball of fire and gas and smoke filled the tower.

Smit paled and faltered. Saryan lunged, his blade passing smoothly through his opponent's breast. He left his sword where it stuck and leapt behind the pillar that supported the main part of the corridor roof as the floor rumbled and shook beneath him and the sounds of crashing stones filled his ears.

Saryan picked himself up off the floor. He turned to see Squire Dedham and Baron Reichenhall in the entrance of the guard room. Valya's linen nightclothes rustled as he maneuvered his body into the corridor. Behind him hurried the guardsmen with buckets of water to extinguish the blaze.

Horror spread over the baron's face as his nostrils filled with the smell of powder and burning timbers. Dust and smoke clung to the sweat of his temples as first he muttered, then shouted, "My guns!" He turned toward Saryan. "Traitor! Filthy spy! You've destroyed my guns!" He reached for his lieutenant's shirt and began to twist it.

"My Lord," shouted Dedham, "it was not Saryan who betrayed you. It was Smit." He pointed at the body on the floor. A wooden beam rested across the man's chest.

Valya followed the squire's gaze and released Saryan.

"But why? He was trusted, well rewarded. Why?"

"He hated Saryan, my Lord, was jealous. He wanted to make it look like Saryan had destroyed the guns so you would kill him."

The baron looked at his lieutenant again. "Is this true?"

"It is my Lord," he said. He remembered Smit's lying and plotting, and how he had hoped to increase his power. It was truer than anyone might suppose, thought Saryan.

Valya Reichenhall pulled at his beard. He had known his captain's ambitions, also his jealousies. That's why he was so useful—because he was known. He wasn't just a pawn, this one, but a rook like Dedham.

And what of Stephen Saryan? What was known of him for certain? The baron's eyes narrowed. "Why should I believe you, Saryan? Who are you that I should believe you?"

The guards murmured as Lady Arla rushed breathlessly into the corridor. She stopped short at the sight of her husband in his nightclothes, the smoke in the air, and the body on the floor.

"What's happened?" she gasped.

"It seems there has been a traitor among us. This is no place for you, Arla," said Valya. He glanced at Saryan. "Or perhaps it is, after all. Your favorite model has put himself in a most compromising position."

"I was explaining that Smit was a traitor, my Lady," said Saryan.

Arla knew she could help him, but why should she lie? How would this help her father's cause? That was after all, the only real reason for her being here, and she did not even know for whom this man worked.

"It is true, my Lord. Master Saryan told me he feared the captain was plotting your death and wanted to seize control of the castle. He said he would tell you of the treachery as soon as he had sufficient evidence."

Reichenhall raised his eyebrows at his wife. It must be true then. Certainly, Arla would do nothing to jeopardize her position or the position of her father.

"So," he said slowly, "both you and Dedham support this story." He looked at Saryan. "I want a full report on this whole affair. Now, come with me to my quarters."

The baron shouted at the guardsmen, "Hurry up and put those fires out. I want it all cleaned up by tomorrow afternoon." He stormed his way past his men toward the south wing.

Saryan exchanged glances with Arla and Dedham. There was no backing out now. All were committed to this deception. He had succeeded. The duke would be pleased.

CHAPTER 8

Settlers

It was dark all around the Biological Research Station. The two scientists rose to enter the low building, taking their chess set with them.

"A very interesting conversation, Joe," said Chris.

"Yes, though a little longer than anticipated. That last story sounded like a movie script. What's his name, the actor with the thin mustache? He would have played Saryan."

"A lot of history makes for good movies and novels."

"It does sound like fiction," replied Dr. Miller.

"My ancient history professor used to say that all history is fiction."

Miller raised his eyebrows, "Fiction? What about facts? You, a historian and archaeologist calling it fiction?"

"Oh, names, places, dates, and so forth, those are factual enough. But to know what was in people's minds and whether what they did or said was right or good—those are judgement calls. The history you read is always prejudiced by the viewpoint of the writer, no matter how objective he tries to be."

"So, what really happened to the baron, Saryan, and the rest? The story you just told me was obviously very richly embellished."

Chris grinned. "Yes, that is what makes it so much fun. Valya had a son but died soon thereafter of what we think was a heart attack. Arla governed with the help of Dedham and Saryan until the boy was old enough to rule. Oh, and Saryan negotiated a very successful alliance with the duke. We suspect that was the real reason why he was sent there."

The old man smiled back and looked westwards to where the sky was still a little golden from the recent sunset. "And next?" he asked.

"Pretty much just more of the same for a long time. The next big thing was industrialization."

Dr. Miller opened the station door and touched the light switch. "That is a story we do not know the end of, I'm afraid."

"No, at least not in our lifetimes."

The folding chairs were returned to their places. The young archaeologist headed for his jeep.

"Nice you could come by," said Miller,

"It's always fun. I'll see you again tomorrow or the next day and we can continue the story." The two men waved as Chris drove away.

Ted Morley leaned against a fence post. He smiled as he surveyed the day's work. Not a root nor stump could be seen in the fields which stretched away toward the water's edge, only patches of grass and an occasional rut where Ted's wagon had stuck in the soft spring earth. With the ground cleared he could now begin plowing and planting. It would be none too soon, either.

The lake's deep blue changed to gold as the sun fell behind the western stretches of the Great Mountains, and black in the shadow of Ruin Island, which brooded in the middle of the water. The lurking remains of ancient stone works were visible there, of little interest now except to superstitious folk and children. Legend had it that it was haunted, full of ghosts, but crows and rats seemed more likely to Ted.

Beyond the island he made out the evening lights of Newtown, where it nestled against the farther shore. On all sides stretched the darkening forest, broken here and there by farms and roads and cottages.

Ted pulled a piece of grass and stuck it between his teeth. He sighed and turned to his wagon. He drove at an easy pace, rough enough on such a road, if it could be called a road, passing trees and meadows, taking note of where future clearing might be worthwhile. Quickstream was filled with the melting snows of the Great Mountains and run-off from spring rains. It bubbled noisily as Ted crossed the new bridge he and neighbor Brown had built.

The cottage lay tucked against a spur of the Lesser Mountains which blocked his land from the view of Caren, the only village on the south side of the lake. Joee ran to him in the shaft of yellow light that came from the open door. The smell of simmering stew and fresh bread wafted after her.

"I'm glad you're back, Mr. Morley," she said with a hug.

"I'm glad to be back, Mrs. Morley," he replied. "But if you don't let me put Sally in the barn, she'll be very unhappy."

He swatted her bottom and walked to the low building, partly hidden by the old forest.

"Okay, but if you don't hurry, I'll be unhappy too. Which is worse?" she called.

"I'll hurry."

They had been married two years. Though they had no children, they were happy with their lives. Under the new law they had claimed enough land to start a good farm and ensure a comfortable future. They were lucky to have this particular area. It had once belonged to serfs of the island barons, and there had been some doubt about who owned it. But after a hundred years of nearly total disuse the state reclassified it as wilderness, open for homesteading, just in time for a new family, or at least a couple who wanted to become a family.

After dinner Ted stretched out in his favorite chair, took a long draw on his pipe, and stared into the fire that danced on the hearth before him. Joee rocked gently in her place, working on an intricate floral needlepoint.

"Neighbor Brown was by this afternoon, Ted."

"Huh. What did he have to say for himself?"

"Oh, the usual. He just wanted to gossip. He and John finished planting their corn. They're ahead of schedule a bit."

"He told me he thought they wouldn't finish 'til next week." He blew some smoke at her. "Anything else interesting?"

"No, just something about some new people in town. 'Going to build a mill or some such thing. Sounds good."

"Yes, I suppose that will be good. New industry. Prosperity." He yawned deeply.

The next morning found Ted guiding his plow in a deep furrow in the field he had finished clearing the evening before. Dew still clung to the grass and robins signaled the beginning of day.

It was towards noon when the young farmer had begun to feel the first stirrings of hunger that he noticed the little group of strangers walking across his field from the east. There were four of them, each much different from the other physically. One was short and fat, another tall and lean, a third tall and large, but with largeness made of muscle that threatened to burst his clothes.

Slightly ahead of these three strode a large man who obviously was the leader. Head and shoulders taller than Ted, he had the air and carriage of a dignitary. He wore a fine brown and red wool suit with a crisscross double check pattern, like what visitors from the city wore to see the country folk in their primitive setting. Ted wasn't sure if the stranger's bulk was the strength of a boxer in his prime or the fat of a rich man who had others do his work for him, but he was sure of one thing—he was no friend.

"'Morning, Neighbor," said the stranger, taking from his mouth a large cigar. "'Name's George. George Stevens."

"Good morning. I'm Theodore Morley. What can I do for you?"

"Oh, nothing in particular. My associates and I are visiting, just looking over the valley. Beautiful country. Yessir, very beautiful. 'Hope you don't mind if we walk across your ground here?" His eyes glinted.

Ted shook his head. "Just stay off the part that's already plowed."

"Sure. Sure. Been livin' here long?"

"About a year. We came under the new homestead laws."

"Homestead laws? I thought all this area was settled back when they were here." Stevens pointed his cigar at Ruin Island.

"Yes. But that was a long time ago. After the plagues the population was low, and then a lot of people left for the new lands that were opened up in the far west. A lot of the valley was left empty. Our farm here was declared wilderness just a year ago. So here we are."

"I see. Congratulations! None of the old owners around to be interested in it, huh?"

"I guess not." Ted felt a little uneasy at the man's questions. He rocked back on his heels and stared toward the island. What had become of the original owners? Surely there were records dating back to that period.

Stevens grinned, "Well, I suppose we'll be movin' on. 'Hope we didn't interrupt your work."

"No bother. Good day."

"Good day." The men walked back down the field toward the shore and the little foot bridge that crossed Quickstream not far from where it emptied into the lake.

Ted looked after them, glanced again at the island, and called to Sally, shaking the reins.

That evening after dinner the Morleys had a visitor. Tom Brown was not as tall as Ted, but his girth made him appear larger. Many years of farming had browned and leathered his old skin. Not all his hair was grey, and what was not was bleached from long hours in the sun.

Tom was one of those people whom everyone knew and who knew everyone. If there was anything important happening anywhere around Caren, Tom was bound to have heard of it and chances were he was involved as well. He seemed agitated that evening as he sat rubbing his knees,

"Get a lot done today?" he asked.

"Pretty much. I've been working right along. More to finish than to start as the saying goes." They all laughed.

"Well now, what I come to say is, well, I'm not sure what I can make of it, or if there's anything to make of it at all. But I was in buyin' some nails at the store today, for the fence down on Smithy Hill—it's comin' along fine. Well, I was there, and Bob tells me, he says, 'Those strangers in town are up to no good,' he says.

"Well, I says to him, 'What strangers are those?' and he says, 'those fellas over there.' And sure enough there are these four fellas a' comin' out of the land agent's office across the street."

Ted waved to get the old man's attention. "Was one of 'em a big, tall man smoking a cigar and wearing real fine city clothes?"

"Yep. Yep. He's one of 'em. Do you mean they've already been out here?"

Ted sat up in his chair and looked over to Joee. Her needlepoint was almost finished. It was a red rose growing out of a tangle of eglantine and lily of the valley. She had dropped it in her lap.

"They were out walking across the fields, but what do you mean by 'already'?"

The old man paused and bit his lip. "Well, after I bought me my nails, I went over to the land agent—a new fella, about thirty, said his name is Smith or Jones or something—well, I went over and asked what the strangers wanted. Close this new guy is, downright close, like diggin' for gold, trying to get something out of him. Anyhow, he says they was lookin' for land to start a business, so I asked if they are the same ones as are going to build the new mill I told Joee about yesterday." They exchanged smiles.

"You see, I hadn't seen 'em before, only heard about it from Bob. Bob hears everythin'. Good man to know. So, as I was sayin', I asked if they was the same ones and he says they are, which made me say to myself, 'see, no reason to get excited after all.'"

Ted put his chin in his right hand. He felt more amusement than exasperation at the old man's circuitous way of telling a story. "But that's not all, right?"

"No. No. That ain't all at all." The old face grew darker. "Then I asks where they want to build the mill and he says, 'on Quickstream.'"

Ted started. "Quickstream? That's my property. 'Flows right down the middle. There's no empty land available."

"Well, that's what I said to this Smith or Jones fella. But he just says, 'can't stand in the way of progress' and mumbles something about laws and claiming open land. I don't know what's goin' on. But I thought you ought to hear about it before they try to pull a fast one."

"Nonsense. They can't take land that we own. I have a deed, and it's not for sale."

But Ted felt a chill. It had been a short year for them on the farm, working from light to dark every day. The harvest from their little garden had been barely enough to carry them through the winter, and even then, they wouldn't have made it without Brown's help. This year they hoped the garden and the sale of the corn from the newly cleared land would keep them. And there might be enough extra to buy a few sheep or a cow. And now to have someone threaten to take it all away . . .

"Sorry to bring bad news."

Tom looked at his friend carefully. "Well, we don't know yet that it's all that bad. We will just wait and see."

"Yep, I suppose so. I'd best be getting home. The wife will be waitin' up." They rose and went to the door, the old man pulling on his coat. "And Ted, no matter what happens, we're with you all the way."

They slapped each other on the back, and the old man went out, mounted his horse, and left. Ted turned to Joee and put his arm around her. Her soft brown hair fell in long waves about her shoulders, framing the round face and hazel eyes. There were lines on her forehead. "They can't force us to sell the farm, or take it from us, can they?"

He pulled her head to his chest. "No, of course not. Tom probably just has his stories mixed up and made big again, is all." He looked across the meadow and the forest to the lake beyond and to the island on the lake. He did not sound convinced.

CHAPTER 9

Entrepreneurs

Leroy Smith had done well at District Headquarters, he thought. Why they should have sent him to an out-of-the-way place like Caren, he did not know. It felt like punishment. He preferred the city or at least the suburbs and had hoped to be assigned to one of the new planning boards in the East. That would have been a plum. He sighed as he stared out the dirty window onto the street.

It was a wide street, wider than many in the city. One would think they could pave it, though, especially in such a wet climate. The clouds had broken, and the midday sun warmed the town. Wisps of steam rose from the street, but still the ground was wet, and the road muddy. Beyond the roof of the store opposite Smith thought he could glimpse a part of the lake.

He turned back to his cluttered desk and stared at the papers. Such a mess! He hadn't been in such a mess in years. There wasn't really much for him to do in Caren. An occasional boundary dispute, quarrels about game rights, and now the matter of settling homestead claims. And of course, the all-important annual inspection to see that the necessary improvements were made to validate recent claims. Amazing that so much paper can be generated by so little work.

Now this big man from the East had really disrupted things. After all, no one had heard of the Reichenhalls for over two hundred years. And now this. Of all the possible complications in land ownership, this was least expected. What to do with the Morleys?

He leaned back in his swivel chair and sighed, removing his eyeglasses, and swinging them by the frames. Oh well, it will work out one way or another. It always does.

There was a knock at the door and Ted Morley entered, a crisp, folded document in his hand. "You wanted to see me," he said dryly.

"Yes, Mr. Morley. I'm glad you are so prompt. It's about Mr. Stevens' claim."

"The claim is nonsense. I'll not talk about it." He turned to go.

"No, wait. Wait just a minute," the agent called. "I must explain the situation. Please sit down." The urgency in the man's voice caused Ted to stop, look a moment at him, and then sit opposite.

Smith folded his hands and began, "You see, I don't think you fully understand the situation, or the benefits if you cooperate."

"All I see is a big-city swindler trying to steal my land after I've worked hard to clear it."

"Yes. Yes, I understand. But there is more. Much more. Mr. Stevens owns a number of large companies in the East as well as some important ones in the West. It happened that on a trip to the coast he passed through this valley. He felt strongly that industry would do well here, especially a flour mill, and later, shipping, which as you know we desperately need.

"He decided then that Quickstream was the best site for his mill, so began a search for the owners in hopes of purchasing it. All this time he hunted until he found one last family of the Reichenhalls who, by good fortune, could prove their identity. Mr. Stevens bought the claim from them, thus entitling him to the land on both sides of the mouth of Quickstream for a distance of two miles in all directions."

"That's all very well," interjected Ted impatiently, "but what about our claim under the homestead law? What about the work I've put into the land? And what about our deed?" He threw the paper he had been clutching onto the table. "There's my deed, Read it. It includes the land Stevens wants. Grazing and farmland—that's how it is classified. And it is mine!"

Smith waved his hands. "I know all about that, Mr. Morley. In fact, I have a copy of your deed right here." He picked up another paper from the stack on his desk. These farmers are such impatient fellows in legal matters, he thought. "Let me finish. Mr. Stevens has offered a very fine reimbursement for your property. Certainly more than it's worth as farmland. With it you can buy more land if you wish. I strongly recommend that you accept his offer."

"Well suppose I just don't want to accept it?"

Smith looked at his guest, So impatient. So stubborn. Why are they all so stubborn? He rubbed his front teeth with his tongue.

"Mr. Morley, not only will the presence of one of the Stevens' companies be a boon to our growth and development; not only will the mill mean added prosperity for the valley; not only will the reimbursement be sufficient for you to purchase other land; but I have here a cable from the District Land Office empowering me to demand a court order seizing the property and turning it over to Mr. Stevens if you don't agree to his terms."

He waved another paper. "I do not wish to invoke this, because it would mean Stevens would be under no further obligation to reimburse you, but if you continue to tax my patience, I will have no choice."

Ted's throat was dry. He trembled as he stood and picked up his deed. "We'll see,'" he whispered.

Leroy Smith watched him go, then smiled grimly. He didn't like getting tough with people, but sometimes one simply had to. He settled back in his chair. Silly stubborn farmers! Don't they recognize progress when they see it? Downright obstinate.

Smith looked out the window to the store on the other side of the street. A weather-beaten old man was haggling with Bob about the price of a small machine with tiny knives and a large wooden crank. A cherry pitter. Remarkable, thought Smith, what modern technology can produce. Then he turned back to his papers.

Otto didn't like his work. As soon as Rich and Joe finished the plans, he would have to start digging the footings, and that was no fun.

He thought back to his last job for Mr. Stevens, They only built a little relay station for his freight company that time, but the old owners put up a real fight. The fighting wasn't as hard as the work, though. The hardpan was just four inches beneath the surface, and he had to dig it!

He peered into the early morning gloom. A fog had rolled in from the lake; only the muffled sounds of the other men talking by the fire broke the deathly silence.

Things were different once, thought Otto, when he was on the railroad gang. That was hard too, but regular, and it seemed better somehow, less tense maybe. If only that foreman hadn't pushed him around. Otto's hands tightened on the shovel handle as he recalled vividly how it felt to twist the foreman's neck. But that was bad. If Stevens hadn't given him a new name and a job and hid him until the search was over, he would have been a tree ornament long ago, he thought. Stevens. There was a strong man. A man you could follow. If only his jobs weren't so hard.

The gloom began to fade and the mists to rise and the fire seemed less bright. Before long he could see across the lake to the surrounding hills, all grey and green beneath the thick canopy of clouds that hovered a few hundred feet above their heads.

"Well," grunted Joe, a thick, squat man with sniffles, "time to get to work."

Rich, his opposite in form but twin in personality, cursed, placed his coffee cup by the fire, and followed to where the two had already heaped a pile of stakes by the stream. Otto didn't know anything about surveying, so picked up his shotgun and held it close. Guarding was better than digging, but it too would be a bore after a while. When it came right down to it, there wasn't anything that wasn't boring after a while.

Half the day went by. Otto was surprised the loud young farmer hadn't come to tell them to clear off like he did the day before. It had been late in the day when they started, and no sooner had they driven the first stake than he came running over the hill waving his arms and shouting about private property. There was almost a fight, but Mr.

Stevens came and set the fellow straight in a calm sort of way, just talking to him. Otto recalled the bright shine of the young man's black hair and the gleam in his eyes and thought, he'll be back, Mr. Stevens. He'll be back, and I'll have to settle with him yet.

The young farmer never came that day. Instead, a fat old man with a pitchfork rode up on a buckboard. "What do you fellas think you're a doin' here? This here's the Morley land. Go on now, get off'n it."

"Hey old man, why are you botherin' us? This land belongs to Mr. Stevens." Otto gestured with his gun.

"Now looky here, I've lived around here longer than you boys been alive, and I know who owns what. The Morleys was here first. You boys're askin' for big trouble, believe me!" With that the old man climbed down from the buckboard and brandished his weapon.

"Old man, we don't want no trouble. Just leave us alone and keep out of other people's business." Otto started to turn as if to call Joe and Rich, but instead jerked to the left and swung the butt of his shotgun into the old man's groin, knocking him to the ground. "I told you to leave! Now I'll have to carry you myself!"

"Blast it, Otto, why'd you have to go and do that? The boss'll be plenty mad," exclaimed Rich, running up from behind.

"You shut up. I'll take care of this my way. Help me put him in the wagon."

The farmer groaned as they lifted him into the wagon bed. Otto turned to the others and said menacingly, "If you tell the boss, I'll twist your little necks! I'll tell him myself if I've got to, but you won't!"

The farmer groaned again. "You shouldn't have hit him so hard. He's an old man."

"I said for you to shut up, see!" He advanced on Rich.

Rich sucked in his breath and backed off.

Otto climbed onto the buckboard and drove it back toward the road. He looked into the bed where the farmer writhed, his arms clutched around his middle. Meddler. If only people wouldn't meddle in others' affairs. Serve the old fool right if he couldn't walk straight again. He stopped at a place in the road where the trees blocked the view in both directions. Dew had collected in puddles along the way and Otto worried the wheels might get stuck in the mud, which was deep in some places from mist and drizzle.

"Okay, old man. I won't kill you, though maybe I should. You just stay off of Mr. Stevens' land. Someone will find you here or your horse will just wander back to wherever you came from."

Otto left the wagon in the middle of the road, the horse munching at grass by the edge and the farmer still groaning softly in the back. He lit off across country, over a hill covered with fresh green grass that flamed nearly bronze as sunlight streamed from rents in the clouds above. On both sides the forest stretched dark and ominous. Otto looked back nervously.

All was as he had left it, yet there was a tense vigilance in the air not entirely of Otto's imagination. He continued his walk. "Strange place," he muttered to himself. "The city's better."

Stevens didn't just build a mill. He built a dock too, right on the mouth of Quickstream. Of course, he brought in laborers—there weren't enough in the valley—and other workers to run the mill and the ferry service he started between Quickstream and Newtown across the lake. All this meant a lot of activity in Caren, men coming and going, supplies arriving from over the mountains and from up Big River. The activity increased even more when Mr. Stevens had the road from Caren to Quickstream widened and improved.

Ted could watch the whole affair from his northern fields by the lake, where they butted up against the Stevens land. He was still angry. He hated to see the buildings go up, despite the profit he made on the sale of the land. Sure, he thought, things are comfortable enough for us, but I sweated over that land and to have some rich easterners come and claim it so high-handedly . . .

Whenever he caught himself brooding about it, though, Ted would remind himself of poor Mr. Brown and the hard time he had had recovering from the blow Stevens' ruffian had given him. No sense people getting hurt over it, he thought. Everyone's all right now.

Things couldn't improve any. It is a good harvest, all are healthy, and the valley is as beautiful as ever.

Ted scratched his ear and smiled. Below him could be heard the bustle of men at work, hurrying to complete the mill in time to handle part of the wheat that had recently been harvested. Lights shone in the gloaming to reveal tents crowded around Quickstream, and the men near them. The last bit of sun touched the tops of the Lesser Mountains in a last burst of glory before being extinguished. Darkness fell on the valley and the lake and Ted began his walk home.

Joee was waiting for him, as always. "You're late, Ted. What was the matter?" she asked.

"Nothing, looking down the valley is all. We had a nice sunset. Dinner ready?" He plopped in his chair.

"In a minute." She sang softly as she set the table.

Afterwards Ted stepped out onto the porch for a minute, thinking idly of the crickets and tree frogs that chirped nearby. Joee followed and put her arm around his waist. It was a chilly night, foreshadowing a long fall and winter. She murmured something and Ted looked down into her eyes, seeing the stars reflected in them.

"I have a surprise."

"What's that?"

"Guess!"

"You found gold in the backyard under the pine tree?"

"No." She grinned as if she had played a good joke, then whispered in his ear, "You're going to be a father."

He stared at her for a moment while the news registered, then leaned to kiss her. The night seemed suddenly much less cold. For a moment the crickets paused to listen while the forest rustled its congratulations. A new generation was coming, and with it a new era.

CHAPTER 10

Businessmen

"Whew! How can you stand it in here?" asked Chris Lowie as he stepped into the humidity of the Biological Research Station. He mopped his neck with a red and green handkerchief, looked around at the pots of flowers, weeds, and gallons of fen water, and fell into an empty swivel chair. The rank smell of decaying plants and rancid water filled his nostrils.

"You get used to it," replied Dr. Miller with a grunt. "I'll be with you in a moment." His old frame was bent over a scanning microscope mounted on one end of the long table that ran the length of the room. Piles of notes, report forms, dried leaves and fungus crowded around him. On a portable table rested an antique typewriter, a half-filled page stuck in it.

"That's that," exclaimed Miller triumphantly. He jotted something on a piece of paper, then turned his chair to his visitor. "No doubt about it, our gribble population is on the increase."

"Gribble?"

"A variety of Limnoria lignorum. They're a tiny wood-boring invertebrate related to the crab. Ordinarily they are strictly a marine animal, but it seems our little valley has grown a fresh-water type. Doing quite well, too."

"I'm thrilled," replied Chris. "Say, I thought you just fooled around with weeds and things, Joe." Chris glanced around the room, crowded with green things and some things not so green.

"That is the main focus. But you can't understand the way plants live without taking a look at the fauna as well." The old man's leathery face looked suddenly indignant. "I'm surprised that a bright young archaeologist like you is not sensitive to evidence from allied disciplines. What are they teaching you boys in college these days?"

"Okay, let's not get into that," laughed Lowie. "We will have to move the chess board outside. It's terrible in here." He waved his hand in front of his face.

Miller put the typewriter on the floor and the two of them moved the table into the shade of the large maple tree. There they set up chess pieces retrieved from an old bag in one of the station's many drawers.

It was a clear day, with fleecy clouds drifting away to the west. The breeze from the lake kept the mid-summer heat from becoming too uncomfortable. At the far end of the lake tall buildings and towers of Wood Village could be seen merging with those of Caren on the right and Newtown on the left. Between them were narrow suburban areas where a few trees still grew to protest the urban sprawl around them. In the middle of the lake sprouted Ruin Island. A new resort hotel was being built on top of the old castle, part of which had been restored.

Nearer to hand stretched the fen, green and lush. On both sides stretched all that remained of the great forest that once filled the valley and covered the mountains. The courts were to decide whether the fen and the woods should be made into a game refuge and park or be sold to the contractors who eagerly coveted them. In either case Miller and Lowie would continue their respective work as long as possible, one tracing the intricate webs of a unique ecology, the other piecing together from their remains the story of a prehistoric people that lived in the forest millennia before.

"Your move," said Chris.

"I know. Don't rush me." The old man made a face. "I'm underpaid and overworked, the department won't give me an assistant, plus the Bureau of Aboriginal Studies sends an archaeologist out here who plays chess like a grandmaster. It's not fair."

Chris laughed. Then he said more soberly, "They turned down your request for help again, huh? That's too bad. 'Sorry to hear it." He thought of the two students he had working for him.

"Yep," muttered Joe, studying his opponent's queen. "They think my reports are important enough to make me send them in triplicate, but they won't even send me a typist to help out."

"Just as well, considering who the poor typist would have to work with."

"Enough of that! They could send a new typewriter while they're at it. And to top it off, next Tuesday I have to appear at a hearing to tell a judge or attorney or somebody what I've found." He moved his bishop two spaces.

A jet overhead distracted Chris's attention for a moment. Then he said, "It sounds exciting. What will you be telling them?"

"The usual. I've been saying for years the lake pollution is approaching dangerous levels. Why, the balance of this whole stretch of swampland has been totally disrupted just since I started work here. You really want to know why the gribbles are doing so well? It's because we have so much decaying wood and other plant life for them to burrow in. You should see some of the other things that are growing in that water."

"Well, Joe," said the young archaeologist, "if you've been saying that for years, why are you just now being called to testify?"

"No one was interested in one poor biologist's complaint. But some big contractor got hold of my reports and is worried the water sports will fall off and no one will want to move lakeside anymore. Money makes all the difference. In some circles I'm a celebrity now."

"All right, Celebrity, your queen is in danger," said Chris, moving a pawn.

The robins in the trees surrounding the research station stopped twittering as a black sedan came to a quick halt in front of the low building. A tall man stepped out of the car and approached Dr. Miller. He had piercing brown eyes, his jaw jutted out at a sharp angle, and his suit, though a little rumpled, was obviously expensive.

The man put out his hand and said, "Good morning. I'm Michael Lowenstein. I think you received my letter, Dr. Miller."

Joe pawed at his pocket as if the letter were there. "Ah, yes. Lowenstein. This is a friend, Chris Lowie."

They exchanged greetings. Lowenstein said, "I wanted to meet you in person and see how your work is coming." He glanced at the chess board.

"The work's fine. The game's off," grumbled Miller, fetching a third chair from the station. "In your letter you say you're concerned about pollution, Mr. Lowenstein."

"Yes. You see, I'm president of Interstate Land Corporation. We're developing the property on Ruin Island, so we are worried about the quality of the environment here. All in the public interest, of course."

Chris felt a wave of disgust. One of those guys, he thought.

"Well, the pollution is there, all right," replied Joe. "It's killing a lot of the wildlife and has disrupted the balance of nature quite a bit, more especially over in the swampland, but out around the island as well."

"I see." Lowenstein's dark eyes flickered. "What do you think is the source of the pollution?"

Dr. Miller considered the question only an instant. "Don't have to look far. Trash from the cities on the lake, pollution from the mines up Big River. The worst offender is probably the paper mill on Quickstream, though. It puts a lot of waste into the water."

Chris thought he saw a faint smile appear on Lowenstein's face.

"Is this hazardous to people?" asked the developer.

"You bet it is. Whenever you start juggling with nature you have to be careful, or you might drop something. And that can be dangerous."

"Do you have plenty of evidence to this effect for the hearing Tuesday?"

"Some," said the old man, rubbing his chin. Work goes kind of slow with no help, but I've some things to say."

Chris wondered why Miller made that remark.

Lowenstein glanced at the archaeologist. "No help?"

"Nope. This young fellow has an excavation over in the forest. Digs up old bones and things."

"You don't have any assistants here?" The man looked astonished. "But your work is so important." He paused a moment. "Perhaps we can do something to help you."

"It would certainly be appreciated," said Miller.

Chris was shocked when he realized what had transpired. After a few minutes of pleasantries and the usual farewells, the visitor left in as much of a hurry as when he arrived.

Chris turned to Joe. "How could you do that?" he asked.

"Now Chris, what do you mean?" The old biologist returned to the chess board.

"You sold out! You let him think you would give support to his cause in exchange for financial aid to your project." Chris was outraged.

Dr. Miller smiled ever so slightly. "It seems that way, doesn't it? Now simmer down and make your move," he added, pointing at the board.

George Stevens IV leaned back in his cushioned chair, lit a dollar cigar, and looked at the rows of portraits on the walls of his conference room. On the left were the faces of his father, grandfather, and great-grandfather, all bearers of the same name and the same features. George thought about his ancestors. Smart men. They took advantage of the times they lived in and built an empire.

The first George Stevens was already wealthy when he came to the valley, but it was from the mills and shipping lines here that his fortune grew to legendary proportions. And that was within a decade. Yet that growth paled to insignificance compared to the growth of the company when the second George Stevens took over. He decided to replace the old grist mill on Quickstream with a pulp and paper mill to make use of the timber that crowded the hills. Each generation was another advance, each son a new success and a new fortune with diversification into manufacturing, wholesaling, and retailing a whole variety of products.

On the right wall were group portraits—the executives of the Stevens' organization, the company men who knew how to get the job done. Now George looked at the dozen men seated at the long table, waiting for his orders and decisions. Good men, he thought, men I can depend on in a crisis.

"Gentlemen," he said, taking his cigar in hand with a flourish, I assume you've all read the government report and the letters from Lowenstein and the others."

"Yes, Mr. Stevens," the men replied in unison. A dozen heads nodded together.

"What do you think? I'm open for suggestions."

There was a pause of several minutes as each man waited for someone else to speak first. At last, a fat bald man in his forties spoke. He was Smith, head of Public Relations. "Sir, I've followed the press reaction to the whole affair and compared our local sales. There appears to be a definite adverse reaction locally. Sales are way off. As long as we maintain a near monopoly it's all right, but if foreign competitors move in, our local and regional markets may dry up."

Stevens leaned forward. "Do you mean to tell me people are actually refusing to buy our products because they think we pollute the lake?"

"Yes, Sir. That's right. It seems largely the fault of the Society for Clean Air and Water. They've been stirring up a lot of publicity, even more than the reporters and columnists themselves, and their lobby at the capital is especially well organized and efficient."

Stevens took a long drag on his cigar, the smoke curling around his massive boxer's body, then fluttering away in the draft of the air conditioner. "Amazing," he said. "And what about our people? We're fighting this every inch of the way, aren't we?"

"Yes, Sir. Senators Jackson and Robins have agreed to sit on any bills that come up in their committees for as long as they can." He paused. "But I'm afraid it's just a matter of time before one of them passes. Legislation might even force us to shut down." Smith cringed when he saw Stevens' expression turn stormy.

"Time? What's time got to do with it? Kelly, how many employees do we have?"

A small owl-faced man said, "About three thousand, Sir. That's in the valley itself, and in directly related companies. Our subsidiaries increase the number to over twice that. Of course, company-wide figures are substantially . . ."

"Enough," interrupted Stevens. "It's here the trouble is, not the rest of the country. Three thousand men and women, Smith." He pointed his cigar at the fat man. "That's three thousand families that would have no paychecks if we closed. Don't these fanatics realize this company is the bedrock of the economy? If we fall, so does everybody else. Have we been telling them that?"

"Yes, Mr. Stevens."

Stevens leaned back again into his chair and sucked on his cigar. That should point them in the proper direction, he thought. We have to have the correct public stance—forceful, but kind, caring, generous. Yes, even righteous.

A soft, high voice interrupted his reverie. "Mr. Stevens," it said.

"Who's that?" asked Stevens, peering down the long table.

"Cranshaw, Sir, Wilbur Cranshaw, Chief of Pollution Control."

Stevens stared at the little man at the far end of the table and searched his mind. Pollution Control? Ah yes, he had it, the new department. A token, a tidbit thrown to the dogs to appease their appetites a few months ago when the bad publicity started. And Cranshaw must be the man from engineering who heads it. What can he want at a time like this?

"Certainly, Cranshaw. I remember you. Good to have you with us. What can we do for you?"

Thin lines appeared on Cranshaw's forehead as he spoke. "It's about our departmental report, Sir. We finished it just this morning and couldn't get copies to the board members prior to this meeting. If you wish I can give you a summary now, however."

There was a pause. "Ah. Very good. that's what I like, gentlemen, a man who won't stop until his job is done. Report away, Cranshaw." Obnoxious little fellow, thought Stevens. This is a public relations matter, not a technical one.

Cranshaw cleared his throat, "Our studies corroborate the government biologist's report concerning pollution levels in the lake ' Furthermore, we have found our plant to be the chief offender."

The room became deadly silent, followed by a low murmur.

"We have also found it thoroughly practicable to install pollution control devices over the course of the next three years that would reduce these emissions significantly. Furthermore, reclamation devices can be attached to these machines to convert the wastes into useful products—fertilizers, chemicals, and so forth. We recommend a subsidiary company be formed to handle such products."

Stevens chewed the end of his cigar. "So, we can make a profit. And eliminate pollution, you say?"

"Yes, Sir, within three to five years."

He thought for a moment. No pollution, no bad publicity, increased sales, and a new subsidiary company selling new products. "I like how you think, Cranshaw. Your plan sounds good. I'll read your report this afternoon when it's ready. You didn't mention cost, though. How about it?"

Wilbur Cranshaw wet his lips. "The cost will be about 50 million dollars over the next three years if we begin immediately."

Loud gasps were heard around the room. The men didn't hear his next sentence. "Of course, the subsidiary could recoup that money after about a decade or so."

Stevens spat out the cigar end he had bitten off, His face was blue as he said coldly, "That's about enough, Cranshaw. Your recommendation is unacceptable. And in the future, you will not present such wild ideas at this meeting. Proposals here must be realistic."

Silence reigned. No one dared speak. George Stevens looked up at his great grandfather's portrait and wondered what he would have done. Finally, a glimmer came to his eye.

"Smith," he said, "who wrote the reports that started this mess?"

"A Doctor Miller. Joe Miller. He's a field biologist who does research at that place on the west end of the lake."

Stevens raised his bushy eyebrows. "West end? What's he doing there?"

"It seems the fen, the swampy area, is some sort of paradise for unusual plants and animals. He's cataloging and studying them."

"Is that why we haven't been able to get timber rights to the place?"

"One reason, yes," said Smith. "But there are other scientists working in the woods, and a lobby of people who want it to be a park and refuge."

Stevens smiled and pulled at his chin. "I see. But this Miller fellow is one of the main roadblocks. He glanced again at the portraits on the wall. "I think I shall pay a visit to our friendly biologist and see how his work is coming along."

CHAPTER 11

Lawyers, Activists, and the Engineer

The resort hotel on Ruin Island was nearly complete. Three stories of plush suites sprawled over the southwest thrust of rock where a landing had been built to handle ferry traffic and the hotel's private boats, rentable, of course, at five dollars an hour or twenty per day. Behind the hotel was a swimming pool, twice Olympic size, in the shape of a lazy clover leaf, accommodating the twists and turns of the island hills. It was heated to a constant seventy-two degrees year-round and already filled for the Lowensteins' personal use until he gave the word to open the hotel to the public.

A short walk over the island was the little museum that conducted tours of the piles of rocks and reconstructed rooms representing old Burg Reichenhall. But it waited empty also, waiting for the owner's command.

Michael Lowenstein smiled as he walked across the hotel roof, planked as a sundeck for pale visitors. Twenty minutes by ferry was all it would take to arrive here from three large cities, commercial centers of a state-wide industrial web. But the rise of ground in the middle of the island cut off the view of all but a small part of that busy blight called urbanization. And if one did want to look across the lake, the only scenery was real scenery—fen, forest, and white-crested mountains in the distance.

Lowenstein had some clever deals to his credit, but this was the crowning achievement. Nothing must be allowed to spoil it.

"May I join you?" asked a short blonde woman approaching him.

"Hi, Fern. Sure."

She leaned against the railing beside him and stared across the lake in the gathering twilight. Fern Knolltree was his private secretary and good friend. They had coddled their island project since its very beginning, worked hard and long for its success, and now shared a feeling of exultation as its opening drew near. They were also pleased about the success of their ecology movement.

"All the press releases are out," she said matter-of-factly. "The courtroom will be packed to the ceiling."

"Good girl. How are the petitions coming?"

"We've almost got enough signatures for an initiative measure. The locals are doing a fine job in the neighborhoods."

"They are always good for that," he said, turning to her. "And at the capital—is your Society for Clean Air and Water busy there?"

"The war's almost won. Joan had dinners with three senators last week, including Sen. Goodman. They're with us too."

He looked down into her pale eyes and noted the same fanaticism he had seen as a youth in the old country during the war. It was a power that could be ignited and directed like an acetylene torch. Anything was possible with that power. As long as it did not get out of hand.

They were a curious pair, he thought. Dark and tall, fair and short, but they worked well together, driving hard toward a common goal. Their motives were different; hers was that deep idealism that thinks itself pure and above evil. His was more honest. All that really mattered was business. Everything else depended on that.

But their immediate purpose was the same, a clean environment, and that was sufficient for the day. As for Fern, she was loyal, energetic, and could be depended on to let him direct her.

"Miller is with us too," he said. "I saw him today. He'll say just what we want him to." There was no reason to tell her about the little deal they made, he thought.

The lake surface turned bronze as the sun began to dip behind the tree lined mountains in the west. Cool air from the north, refreshing during the hot day, but chilly in the evening, drove them from the roof and into the hotel beneath. Marta Lowenstein was in the lounge already. She had dark features like Michael. Her hair was in disarray, and she slumped a little in the booth where she sat. Her hand quivered as she lifted a glass to her lips.

Michael turned on the lights at the switch near the door and shuddered a little to see his wife. "I thought you were going to stay out of here," he said to her.

"So, I lied," she replied, and fired a glance at Fern. "Another strategy meeting?"

Michael nodded to his secretary, and she left discreetly. He maneuvered his way past the tables and potted plants to sit beside his wife.

"Your jealousy is unwarranted," he said truthfully. "Fern and I work together on the hotel and on the ecology movement, but that is all." He paused. "For one thing, she's too short." They looked at each other for a moment, then burst into laughter.

"You do look awfully funny together," said Marta.

She poured him a scotch and water. A few minutes passed in silence. "You know, Michael, if ever I really believed what I sometimes suspect about you, I wouldn't be sitting here drinking."

"No?"

"No. I would be at the newspapers telling them everything I know about your phony pollution campaigns, how they are all just a front and a cover to make sure your precious little resort isn't in danger."

"Don't you think the people who matter already know why I am so zealous?" He spat the words out.

"Sure," she said, gulping from her glass. "But what about little fuzz-heads like Fern baby? They think your chief concern in life is the health and prosperity of the common man—in a clean environment. Suppose they all found out you don't care at all?"

Michael thought of the fanatic gleam in Fern's eyes. "My Dear Marta, it wouldn't work. They wouldn't believe you. The only result would be more publicity for the movement and ultimately for the hotel.

He raised his eyebrows. She smiled in return, then laughed. "We have our rough times together," said Michael Lowenstein, "but we get along. In fact, we get along very well indeed."

"A pleasure to make your acquaintance, Mr. Stevens," said Joe Miller courteously. "Chris, bring our guest a folding chair."

Soon they were all seated in the shade of the great maple outside the Biological Research Station. It was unusually hot. When little trickles of sweat ran down their faces a soft breeze from the lake would stir and refresh them.

"Let me get right to the point," said Stevens, a smile cracking his face. "I've heard of your reports on how the lake water is becoming polluted and all the wildlife is dying."

"Excuse me," interrupted Miller. "That is not quite what my reports say. I have sound evidence of pollution, and many species are being adversely affected by it. Others, however, are flourishing."

"Oh. Well, in any case a lot of people are concerned about what you've said. And, of course, as a public-spirited citizen, so am I. How serious do you feel the pollution is?"

"Quite serious, really. As I said, many species of plants and animals are perishing, others flourishing. The entire balance of nature in the lake and on the shore is being altered. One type of life or resource depends on another in a complex chain from the least plant to the greatest animal, man included. Change any one part of the chain, and all the other parts are thrown out of kelter."

"I see," said Stevens darkly. "But what about people? Are they endangered also? I mean, really?"

"Naturally. Not so directly as the fish, perhaps, but just as certainly."

George Stevens hummed a moment, looked across the lake to where plumes of white smoke could be seen hovering over his mills and factories. "And what's the chief source of pollution, do you think?" he asked casually.

"There are many sources," replied Miller, glancing at Chris. "I think the chief one has been the cities. Too much sewage." Stevens raised his eyebrows. "But they are building improved treatment plants, so that won't be a problem much longer. The big industries are probably the next-worst offenders, mainly for chemical pollution. The bare mountains in the east where too much lumber has been removed contribute heat pollution—the water in the run-off doesn't have a chance to cool before reaching the lake. There are other offenders, too, but those are the main ones."

"Heat pollution?"

"Yes, the mean temperature of water coming off areas that have been clearcut is higher. If the mean temperature of the lake rises, some types of fish have difficulty surviving."

"I see." Stevens stood, put his hands in his pockets, walked in a narrow circle. The old man has got to be reached somehow, he thought. "Dr. Miller, I'll be perfectly frank with you. I've done my very best to eliminate the waste from my plants, or at least to clean it by the time it reaches the lake. I have a team of technologists working on the problem day and night, but the whole thing just goes too slowly for my liking. And the expense is frightful.

"At our present rate of improvement, it will be fifteen or twenty years before we can reach the level of purity we want, allowing for technological advances and for the money it will cost." He paused.

"I know how it is to work with low funds. You see the pitiful state of things here." Miller gestured around him.

That's it, said Stevens to himself. That's the key! "We seem to be in similar situations, Dr. Miller. The public expects results from both of us but doesn't provide us with the resources we need. I need time to develop and to implement new equipment, you need money to build up your laboratory."

Joe Miller smiled and nodded.

"How long do you think we can wait before it becomes urgent to install purification equipment in our plants?" asked Stevens.

"We need it immediately, of course. But it can't be done until it can be done, right?"

Stevens sighed. "No, it cannot. Tuesday at the hearing, if all goes right, we'll both get the dogs off our necks." He glanced around at the station and waved his hands expansively. "And maybe there's something I can do to help with all this. After all, we're fighting the same fight, aren't we?"

"The very same, Mr. Stevens. Struggling to make the world a better place. Industry is necessary for prosperity. Cleanliness is not just next to godliness; it is necessary for good living. I think our goals are the same."

Chris watched the big man leave in his limousine. He turned to the old scientist and tipped his head. "You did it again, Joe. Now he thinks you're on his side."

"He does, doesn't he?" replied the old doctor, a subtle smile gradually appearing. "Maybe I am."

Chris threw his hands up into the air, "But you can't support either one. You're a scientist, don't you see? You are committed to neutrality in this sort of thing. And even if you weren't, you couldn't support one of the worst of the polluters."

"Why not?" Joe sat down and crossed his legs. "The day after that little conversation with Lowenstein our department received a check for three thousand dollars earmarked for this project. Then a note came from the boys upstairs saying they had suddenly decided that my work is so important, they would increase my allotment and recruit two assistants and a secretary. They didn't say how much pressure it took to make them decide that, but look at the results, man! Think what we can do here now! And if Stevens helps too, all the better."

Chris remained standing. "But what are you going to say Tuesday at the hearing? Someone will be disappointed, and plenty angry."

"We will see about that," replied Joe. "As for what I will say, I will just say the truth. That's all." He stared at the maple tree for a moment, then said, pointing at the chess board, "And for heaven's sake, sit down. It's your move."

Wilbur Cranshaw shuffled the drawings on his desk, some from his department, some from accounting. They were diagrams of treatment and purification machines, as well as charts of effluent flow, cost effectiveness ratios, depreciation rates. He ran his hands through his sparse dark hair and cursed softly.

Years, he thought. These have been feasible for years, and technicians have wanted to install them. This one—design seventeen— in the files for twenty-two years, a working model in the garage, and no one even bothered to look at it. Design fifty-four, produced two months ago when they finally created the department. I sent Stevens a memo saying that he should see it. Cheap to install, inexpensive to operate, sixty-two percent effective. He didn't even reply.

He stuffed the papers into a black attaché case and glanced at the clock. One hour until the hearing. His fingers were trembling, "They completely ignore me and my department," he muttered aloud, "but now that they're in trouble they want me to bail them out."

He read again the little handwritten note that had come in the inter-office mail the day before. "Wilbur, we want you to testify tomorrow at one o'clock. We know you will do just fine. Tell them how impossible the anti-pollution drive is at present, how earnestly we want to clean up our waste, how expensive it is, and how frantically we're working on it. I am sure we can find some additional resources to help you and your department. Good luck, G. Stevens IV."

Wilbur wadded up the note and threw it in the grey-green waste basket that stood in the corner.

"'Testify how frantically we've been working.' I'll say frantically," he said again aloud. "Frantically to get people to think we're working frantically. Testify how expensive the devices are at present—use a fraction of your profits and they won't cost anything at all. So, the share price goes down for a while, so what? It will come back up again."

It was his job that was on trial that afternoon, he thought. A promotion or a quiet dismissal, that was the choice. He had to say what the company wanted, no more, no less. He took a deep breath, looked around his small office, and gripped the handle of his attaché case. Whatever happens, he is ready.

CHAPTER 12

Scientists

The first session started promptly at nine o'clock Tuesday morning in the largest public chamber of the county courthouse. Fern's Society for Clean Air and Water had publicized the event and the room was filled. An overflow crowd milled in the hallway and protestors with signs marched around outside. The three tall windows on the east side of the room were opened to let a breeze into the stuffy place, but with so many warm bodies, already it was uncomfortable.

The county attorney and recorder were seated at a long oak table in front. In the first row sat Fern, Joan Brandon, Lowenstein, their lawyers, Stevens, his vice-presidents, their lawyers. Behind them sat wives and witnesses, experts in various fields who had studied conditions in the lake and the mills. Joe and Chris were among them.

The county attorney was a thin man with narrow features and an eyelid that twitched when he worried. His black hair was silver at the temples. He lifted his gavel once and said in a voice already fatigued with the affair, "This hearing is now in session. Our purpose here today is to discover whether a court order should be requested to halt operations of the George Stevens Company's paper and other plants on Quickstream in this county due to possible excessive water pollution.

"All participants will bear in mind that this is not a court, and we will not be bound by courtroom formality. As presiding officer at this hearing, I will put all questions to witnesses called. However, anytime either of the two principal parties involved wishes to pursue a matter, they may ask my permission to do so.

"We will begin with a statement from the Society for Clean Air and Water, at whose insistence this hearing was called."

Fern stood, took a seat on the left side of the table, and identified herself. "The Society," she said, "was founded a year and a half ago by Mrs. Brandon and myself when it became apparent to us that living conditions along the lake are deteriorating swiftly. A number of people have helped us, including Michael Lowenstein, a prominent local developer." She smiled at her boss, and he nodded in return.

The county attorney yawned as Fern continued. "In recent months studies by experts have shown a large amount of the lake's pollution to come from the Stevens' plants. We've asked a representative sample of these experts to testify here today, as listed on the paper we gave you this morning."

The attorney waved a piece of paper in front of him. "Yes, I have it here, though I'm not sure we will have time to hear them all," he said.

A blank look passed over Fern's face as if she were willing herself not to hear his remark. She continued, concluding with an urgent appeal for the purification of the world, that the coming generation might grow up in a wholesome environment, that mankind, nature, even the universe might be preserved.

Lowenstein shifted his weight and thought, Fern sounds not just rehearsed, but almost hysterical. The attorney looked disinterested, even bored, he thought. You must be a fanatic or a fool to enjoy listening to another foolish fanatic's rant. Lowenstein decided the attorney was neither.

Several other men and women were called upon to speak. The hour hand crept around the clock on the west wall. Chris crossed his legs, squirmed in his seat, crossed them again. He felt a throbbing in his right hip he knew came from sitting too long on a hard chair in hot weather. He wished he were back in the forest, digging.

The county attorney made a pencil mark on the sheet in front of him. "Will Dr. Joseph Miller please come forward?" he asked. The recorder's hands floated over her machine. Joe took his place. "Dr. Miller, please describe the nature of your work, your findings, and in particular the report you filed in April of this year."

Someone coughed. A puff of cool air came in the window and the crowd breathed a little easier. Joe began, "I conduct botanical and zoological surveys of wildlife in and around the lake, paying particular attention to the interplay between different species. That's my specialty, ecology. I've been stationed at the government project in the swampy area known as the fen at the west end of the lake for about three years now, and it has become apparent to me that the number and types of creatures in the water are changing in direct relation to the increased concentration of wastes in the water."

"Please explain," said the attorney. Lowenstein smiled.

"You see, all life is dependent on other life forms and ultimately on non-living resources for their maintenance. As conditions change, climate for instance, in response to the variations in the earth's motions and the sun's activity, plants and animals must adapt to the new conditions or die. This is the essential mechanism in evolution. Those creatures adapting to changed conditions survive to form new species as the old ones perish. Man has adapted by improving his technology and industry; in fact, most of our environment today is cultural, that is, man-made.

"But technology affects the rest of nature as well as man. That means that man is a part of the natural conditions to which other wildlife must adapt. Deforestation in some parts of the world, for example, has led to erosion and loss of habitat, in turn leading to the death and extinction of numerous species.

"Significant to note, however, is that as the old ecosystem passes, a new one appears—a deforested area turned steppe soon harbors steppe-type wildlife. Except in science-fiction novels about nuclear war, I'm afraid there is no such thing as destroying the 'balance of nature'; nature finds a new balance, which she would do anyway, even without our help."

Joe sniffed and looked at Stevens, who now was smiling. Lowenstein looked uncertain, while Joan had a vacant expression like that student in the back of the class who has no idea what the lesson is about.

The attorney glanced at his paper and said, "Let me see if I have understood you correctly. Are you saying there is no danger from pollution—except, of course, as already established, the possible medical danger due to high toxicity for swimmers?"

"Not exactly. Continued pollution will destroy wildlife in the lake. The point is that other wildlife will take its place." Now Stevens and Lowenstein both looked confused.

"The real question is what kind of balance we want—it cannot be as it was in the past. It never is. A fundamental principle in evolutionary science is that natural conditions never entirely duplicate themselves. We can, however, direct conditions to a limited degree in order to influence what sort of wildlife, what sort of living conditions we want, at the same time preserving our industries and factories, since these are necessary to us for our continued enjoyment of whatever wildlife we manage to have."

The attorney interrupted, "I see. Could you tell us about your report, Sir?"

Doctor Miller shifted in his seat and looked at his knee. "In my report I explained that numerous species of flora and fauna, specifically fish and mammals, are showing marked decreases in their populations. At the same time others are increasing, notably parasites, crustaceans, and reptiles."

"May I sum up your statement then by saying that pollution is the cause of a change in the pattern of animal and plant life in the lake? And that this change can be modified?"

"Yes."

"How might this modification, this environmental direction be achieved?" asked the attorney.

"By introducing other species into the lake and testing their success, by breeding existing species to find hardier strains, and by avoiding excessive pollution in the future. Reforestation measures already in use will be helpful also."

The biologist glanced again at Stevens. There was no smile there, but no frown, either. The industrialist wasn't sure whether he had been supported or betrayed but suspected it might be the latter.

After the county attorney recessed the hearing for lunch, Chris said in a low voice, "Joe, the audience might have found you a little confusing."

"Maybe, but you understood, didn't you?"

"Of course. How about your two new friends? I don't think they could tell whose side you were on."

"That's just it. I am not on anyone's side but my own. Who cares what they think? I said what I wanted to say. I said the truth. If it so happens that each heard what he wanted to hear, plus some things he didn't . . ." Miller shrugged his shoulders and began to move toward the aisle. "Besides, I had a note from the department this morning. A gift of ten thousand dollars has been received from George Stevens for support of the lake research station. It's too late for either side now."

The old man grinned, nudged his young friend, and said, "Let's go get something to eat."

When the hearing reconvened the tension in the room was noticeably less. It's always that way, thought the attorney, a good meal and a rest and everything is better. It even seemed cooler. He looked out the tall windows at the green lawn and trees and carefully manicured shrubs of the county building. A little further away was twenty-third street, now choked with traffic, as motorists struggled to get back to work or home to lunch or downtown to shop. New high rise business offices and apartments blocked the view of the lake that only a few years ago the county headquarters workers had enjoyed.

Everyone was in place. There were no new faces but one, a nervous little man in the second row, clutching a black attaché case.

The attorney banged on the desk. "We will now hear a representative of the George Stevens Company and a number of experts they've asked to testify."

Stevens' man gave his speech without emotion or fervor, fifteen minutes of cold water from an open tap. "To sum up," he said, "our company is deeply concerned for the welfare and health of the community and is committed to taking all necessary steps toward the improvement of our environment. As others describe these steps in detail, it will become apparent to all what vast amounts of time, energy, and money have gone into our programs. We will also discuss the plans we have for the future and the factors that inhibit the immediate realization of our objectives."

"Thank you," sniffed the attorney.

There was rustling among the audience before the next witness began his testimony. Why do public buildings, schools, and churches always have such hard benches, wondered Chris. Stevens didn't have so many witnesses as his opponents, but they seemed more verbose, dragging on with their carefully rehearsed speeches. They said much the same things as those who had preceded them in the morning, only now the facts were cited as support for Stevens' position. Chris blinked repeatedly to keep from dozing.

Wilbur Cranshaw was last to speak. "Yes, Sir, I am Chief Engineer of the Pollution Control Department at the Stevens Company. We're responsible for new developments in waste control and treatment devices, also for their implementation in the various plants." He pulled at his collar. It was too tight. He had known it was too tight when he tied his tie but was too distracted to change shirts.

"Describe your success in the development of new control devices, Mr. Cranshaw," said the attorney.

"The first such machines were planned twenty-three years ago. They were crude, of course, inefficient, and frightfully expensive. Considerable progress has been made since then, including the development of less expensive, though still cost-prohibitive ones.

Important in all this has been the growth of a systems management plan for organizing and directing our operations in this area.

"None of these plans has yet been put into practice, but the best available projections suggest that the purification and monitoring equipment would be about seventy to eighty percent effective. With the fully developed systems management plan, this efficiency rating would increase to about ninety percent, an improvement of about ten points."

Why did he say that? Anyone could see that the difference was about ten points. Depending on how much "about" was. Wilbur felt a pain in his forehead. The room seemed to float around him like a dream dimly remembered. He pulled at the collar again.

George Stevens muttered something to the man next to him.

The attorney said, "Then these developments could essentially eliminate pollution from the Stevens' plants."

"Yes, Sir. There are theories that point toward a nearly hundred percent purification, but they are not yet realizable and remain only theories."

"Why haven't the existing plans been carried out?"

The pain in Wilbur's head grew more acute. He felt as if he were strangling. He glanced over at his boss, now strangely distorted in his troubled vision. That's strange, thought Wilbur, he looks like a fish, making faces at me, fat, bubbly fish faces.

"Too expensive," said Cranshaw hoarsely. That was what he knew he had to say to keep his job. His eyes ached and he rubbed them. "The cost has been far too great. Impractical." His vision blurred again. His head began to throb. There was no breeze from the open windows now, only still, dead air, in the middle of summer, in the middle of a heat wave. "And no one in upper management listens to us."

"How was that again?" asked the attorney, leaning forward in his chair.

Wilbur turned to the attorney and noticed his eyelid was quivering. "No one ever listens to us, Sir. We've been telling people to put in our equipment for years, long before they created the 'Pollution Control Department', but they don't even come look at our plans. And yes, it is expensive, but the costs can be recouped over time. We checked with the Accounting Department just to be sure."

There was a burst of excited talk in the hearing room. Stevens' mouth opened wide, and his cigar dropped onto his lap. A brash newsman jumped up to take a flash picture of the little man in the chair. Joe Miller poked his elbow into Chris's ribs and chuckled. And all the while the county attorney banged his gavel, calling for order.

It was as if the tension and worry of the day, and perhaps of the months of preparation preceding it, had all burst loose in that moment when one nervous man said what he thought because his collar was too tight.

Finally, the room was silent again. The attorney shot a dirty look at the newsman who had taken the picture. "Do you mean, Mr. Cranshaw, that your department has been trying to implement pollution control measures, but has met with opposition from the company's leadership?"

"That's right." His collar was still tight, but his headache was suddenly gone. He opened his attaché case and withdrew some papers. "Here are charts of cost projections, efficiency ratios, designs. If over the next five years a part of the company's profits were put into this project rather than into marketing or some other area, pollution could be effectively eliminated."

A surge of exultation shook Lowenstein. His own expert witnesses had not accomplished as much as this one man. He nodded jubilantly to Fern.

The rest was anticlimax. There were no more bombs to be dropped, just pieces to be picked up, threads to be tied off before the county attorney gave his decision. When Wilbur finished, he could see his dismissal engraved in Stevens' eyes. He wondered what would become of him, but then thought, there are other companies, ones willing to recycle a used pollution control expert. Something will turn up.

The attorney did not take any time to deliberate. He said, "It seems clear to me, Mr. Stevens, based not just on testimony but also the documents that have been submitted, that you have hindered pollution control efforts in your company. You may think that paying a fine will get you off the hook, but that would not really solve the problem.

"You probably should be prohibited from continuing operations. This would pose a hardship for a great many people, however, especially your employees. Therefore, if you will agree to implement the existing plans presented to you by your own Pollution Control Department, I will not ask the courts for an injunction. Of course, the project will be supervised by county and state representatives to see that it is begun immediately. Do you agree?"

Stevens moistened his lips. He had lost. The expense would be monumental and share prices would plummet, but better this than being closed and picketed and having to make the changes anyway. "Despite the difficulty and expense it will impose, we will consider the question at an emergency board meeting tomorrow and deliver our answer to you as soon as possible."

Chris moved his rook to king's bishop six. "Check." Joe grunted and wiped his forehead with a blue handkerchief.

A male voice from the research station called out to ask where the methylene blue stain had been put. Joe told him, then said to Chris, "The new kid's all right, if only he could learn to keep track of things. At times I wonder if it wasn't easier without him." He looked at the board. "All right, I give up. It's hopeless to try any longer. Just wait— someday I'm going to beat you and then you won't be so smart-alecky."

Chris laughed as they reset the chess pieces for another game. Summer had almost passed from the valley. The first touch of fall color had appeared on the hillsides. The morning mist held a crisp chill that hinted at another long winter. But afternoons were still hot, and a much-appreciated breeze brought ripples to the blue water and threw an occasional drop on vacationers and tired scientists by the shore. The great stone called Ruin Island rested serenely in the lake's middle.

Joe followed Chris's gaze. "Beautiful, isn't it?"

"Yes. I was wondering again how it must have looked to the people who lived on the island centuries ago, or in the forest," Chris said.

Surrounding the valley stood the hills, some now bare where lumbermen had recently passed through, others covered with houses, but most still with at least some woodland. Rivers emptied into the lake after their long trip from the distant mountains. The fen was quiet.

"Well, you filled in a lot of details about those people when we talked about Ratu, the Tarmians, the Reichenhalls, and the rest. I appreciate the history lessons. Some details are different, no doubt, from age to age," said Joe. "The world, the whole universe, is constantly changing, but I think we are seeing essentially the same scene that was here long before us. Nature, the natural world, in all its glory."

He paused and added a little more quietly, "You know, Chris, I think mankind was put here to take care of this world, to take care of nature, and to enjoy it. God made us stewards over His creation and I think He will hold us accountable for how well we take care of it."

The archaeologist tipped his head. "God? After all that talk of science and evolution, I thought you were an atheist."

Joe chuckled. "No. Science is just our way of trying to understand His creation. And evolution is just one mechanism of change, one of His tools for creating. No, atheism is a vanity for academics who spend all their time spouting pet theories and promoting their books. And an excuse for those who read those books to justify their own misbehavior.

"Anyone, including and maybe especially a scientist, anyone who immerses himself in the real world will come to know there must be a God, there must be a Creator, for all this," he gestured around him.

"This did not come about by chance. If we see a different valley now than did our ancestors, maybe it's because we look with different eyes. They were a lot closer to the world around them. Man has been so successful technologically he has become detached from it."

"You have a good point there," interjected Chris.

Miller nodded, continuing with hardly a pause, ". . . and arrogant! Of course, we can and do make changes to our houses, to our immediate environment, to our little cocoons. And man can certainly mess things up, for a while anyway, until nature adjusts and repairs it. If there have been changes to the valley since our ancestors, that's what they are."

"Yes. That's one of the striking things about studying ancient history. Life is so short. It skews our perspective on the world. We only know our brief time here and the environment during a moment of earth's history. Our lives are the blink of an eye."

Joe smiled slyly at Chris. "I suppose that's one of the paradoxes of nature. Yes, things are constantly changing, yet somehow it is always the same. And always so exquisitely beautiful. There is only One who can make real changes, permanent changes on a grand scale, a geologic or cosmic scale, and that's God, using the laws and mechanisms He built into the world when He created it in the first place."

The old man fell silent and contemplated the chessboard with his friend, while a pair of sparrows held conversation in the maple tree above them, perhaps commenting in bird language about the odd humans below. The tree seemed to murmur something in return. The sparrows flew away, but still the tree murmured and whispered to itself in the breeze, nodding its branches as if falling asleep, the whispers fading to a gentle snore.

Postscript

The author grew up near Portland, Oregon, at that time surely one of the most beautiful cities in the world, except for one thing. The Willamette River running through the middle of the city was by the 1950s so polluted with urban sewage, farm runoff, and industrial waste that it was not only unsafe to swim in, but the historically very large salmon runs had also dwindled to non-existence. The water was so bad even fish could not live in it!

Concerted efforts by citizens, industries, and state and local governments during the 1950s, '60s, and early '70s accomplished a miracle: the river was cleaned and restored! The salmon returned. It is possible to make use of natural resources, live happy and productive lives, and still be good stewards of the wonderful world around us. This book was written about 1972.

Also by Roderick Saxey:

The Federalist: Excerpts with Commentary

All Enlisted: A Mormon Missionary in Austria During the Vietnam Era

Turning the Hearts: Counsel for my Distant Descendants

The Trillium Girl

Coming soon:

Growing Up Tough

Improve the Moment